Loa's Secret

Table of Contents

Chapter 1

Loa had a secret, and like most things that were hers, she couldn't wait to share it. The problem wasn't so much who to tell as it was when to tell them. She knew Derig and Keia couldn't be far away. Perhaps they were near the front of the line, or maybe further behind, somewhere on the road that curved around the wall of Lantus Crater and back down into the valley below. The road dropped sheer down to Loa's left, and today it was peopled with hundreds of colonist families—mine workers and their children dressed in dull sagging colors, yawning and muttering as they waited for a chance to enter the Corporation complex, and submit their petitions.

Though Sekris had only the barest atmosphere, the slow artificial sunset was pleasant enough, sinking into a brilliant liquid yellow with colored branches over the vast dome-shield, reminding everyone just how slow the line was moving. Loa had been holding her father's hand for what seemed like days, and was running out of things to think about. The air was warm and smelled of drill foam, the heavy lubricant her father helped make for the Breach Pit, the focal point of the Gevroh Corporation's mining operation in the center of the crater. The rhythmic churn of the pit's eight-headed Master Drill could be heard clearly, far away in the electric twilight.

The best part about having made it this far was that Loa could see the company store. It was still a good way off; the drop-steel front wall closed and locked like the eye of a sleeping robot, but a little closer and she would be able to see the wonderful posters that covered its surface. Inside the store was bright and tidy, and it smelled nice too, with polished burwood shelves and clear glass cases for delicious candies like Glow-Ups, which were her favorite, and Liquings, not to mention those amazing puffy Gel Figs... The pictures filled her mouth with water even though she had never tried one. There were other pictures too—NiteSite goggles so kids could play like real tunnel miners, mini laser picks and authentic mine poles, hauler boots, gloves, dry-suits, and even a few pictures of real live kittens that were kept in a basket near the ceiling—Loa had got to hold one once. But her favorite was the Gevrider, the only Terrain Contact Vehicle the Corporation made for children. The poster at the back of the store showed it in action, under the words *penultimate freedom*, which Loa was sure meant even better than ultimate. The Gevrider was sleeker, faster, and a lot more powerful than the bumpy tasking carts she would ride to work on her assigned days; its cabin was small, but with plenty of room for four adventurers on an important mission, though it was too expensive for any colonist family she knew of, and she had never seen it outside the poster.

Loa scratched at the yellow scarf on her head and glanced up at her father. A thin man with wispy hair whose eyebrows pinched in the center, Marren Dantrue had lost his wife in a mining accident six years back when a tuning pan flipped over spilling hot metal on everyone below. Loa had been splashed—she was only three at the time, and had suffered a small round burn on her head where the hair wouldn't grow back—she'd worn her yellow head scarf ever since. Once a year Marren was compensated for the loss of Anora Lisa Dantrue with a small box of copper barter tokens for the store, and a letter reiterating that the family's ration of what passed for bread and vegetables—barkrolls and rubeet, would be reduced, reflecting fewer family members than originally registered. The tokens this year had bought them a few nice things, including a stash of Glow-Ups for Loa, of which there were still three left at home.

Loa could barely remember the day she lost her mother, but her older sister Henya, who was almost ten at the time, didn't hold up so well. A once promising machine cadet, she started causing all sorts of trouble, eventually landing herself in the dreaded Detention Center deep underground. So each year on Petition Day Loa's father brought the meticulously filled out form to review Henya's case, and waited in line. Together they'd hoped that Imperial officers, having stepped in to oversee Gevroh business these last two years, would be lenient, but their previous appeals had been denied. The Empire would not make exceptions for infractions of vandalism, though the officers promised Henya was being well taken care of, fed and tutored in many technical skills. But Loa still missed her, and she felt a stir of excitement when she caught sight of the carefully folded document her father clutched to his chest.

"We'll see Henya soon?" she asked. "If they sign it I mean."

"Of course, Petal."

It was a question they had gone over many times. On Tasking Days, when children were required to work, Loa missed her sister more than ever—and the next Tasking Day was approaching fast. Henya had made a good partner; the job of scraping or sorting was miserable and difficult without her.

Releasing his daughter's hand to wipe the sweat against his colorless trousers her father scowled at the head of the line, as though afraid he might have missed something. Loa slumped a bit and looked down. She was rather small for her age, with untidy dark hair that reached halfway to her narrow shoulders and soft blue eyes. In fact she stood not much higher than her father's waist, though she assured her friends this was because he was very tall.

The man in front of them was arguing with his son, a sinewy boy who must have been at least seventeen.

"You said every petition would get a fair review. How can it be fair if the Empire leaves?" The boy had a raspy voice and a sooty complexion, as though he already spent most of his days in the exhaust tunnels. His father was slightly plump and red in the face, with patchy white hair and a mustache that twitched like a dust frond in the wind.

"Look Joff, I'd not take those Freezone broadcasts too seriously. This isn't the center of the Imperium, this is Rim world space—Gevroh Sekris is no more important than any other rock in this sector. The only reason we've had an Imperial hand out these past two years, is because General Traig's fleet hasn't been missed yet!"

Joff looked unmoved. He hunched in to continue with a hissing whisper. "Rim world space IS part of the Empire father, where do you think the ore gets shipped to?! Most of it goes to the Core worlds! So don't tell me miners' rights aren't worth protecting. The Sanctor himself should be here! If the Imps pull out and abandon us, Gevroh's thugs will crack right down again, and it will be worse than it was before!"

Joff's father was red in the face. "That's my boy," he grinned and nodded at Marren. "He's got some spark in him. Kids these days need to understand there's war out there—Imperial fleets follow Imperial orders. We thank them for their service, but it was only a matter of time."

"I understand that, but I wish they could stay too," Marren sighed. "At least until they've heard us out."

Loa squeezed his hand. "Weren't we going to ask them to stay?" she inquired.

"No, Petal, well yes." He smiled and squatted down to look at her. "I'd like to remind them of everything the Liaison promised. We're not ungrateful; the food's been cleaner since they arrived, and less accidents. But if they leave now, things might go back to the way they were, and we don't know what that means for Henya." He rubbed her cheek with his thumb. Marren had always believed in sharing the truth with her, and Loa was pretty sure it was better that way. Even bad things were a lot less scary when they were 'unrolled' as he called it, and they could talk over each piece of news on its own.

Her father's hands on her shoulders made her sleepy, and though she tried to keep up as he went into his talk about corporate abuses and the need for solidarity among Rim world settlers, she woke a moment later as he stood up.

"Petal, I can't carry you right now. Another hour or so, and you can rest again; the line is moving."

Feeling hazy but glad to hear it she squinted ahead and found the column had begun to shuffle forward. They were still a few hundred people from the complex entrance, but at this rate the store would be approaching quickly. She could see children already gathered around the front, banging and grasping at the shop doors with dust gloved fists and pale fingers.

Marren followed her gaze and frowned. "They haven't opened yet, Petal, and you know we don't have time for treats."

Loa nodded with conviction. After all she still had three Glow-Ups at home, and those other children probably didn't have any. She sighed as she watched them, feeling it was important to share the extra Glow-Ups with her friends, Keia especially, and maybe Derig, but not until it was time to tell them her secret.

"The ration carts should be coming by soon—got your key?" Marren asked.

Loa reached into her little dust-vest and pulled out the black angular chit that was fastened to a cord around her neck. It was smooth and featureless, save two tiny white dots near the bottom that meant her portion would be small, child size until she was ten.

But the carts never came. The line all but stopped, and several hours later a squad of Imperial soldiers made their way down the road, passing out tokens. Everyone received a few, three or four, and although Loa was passed over unnoticed her father was quick to give her one. The soldiers' gleaming silver armor shone in a sudden artificial dawn as melodious tones of "The Emperor's Way" swam and boomed out of the ground all over the crater.

In the midst of a second group of Imperials walked a tall woman with dark hair tied back and a deep blue uniform. She spoke to the line, and seemed to be repeating herself. "The Emperor thanks you for your support and understanding; our fleet is needed for the Incursion, and will be leaving tomorrow under emergency protocols. The Emperor thanks you for your support and understanding," She spoke loudly and the words were crisp; Loa enjoyed the sound of her voice. The woman looked down at her as she passed and there was a flicker of anger across her face, but just as quickly she had moved on and was begging the forgiveness of the families behind them.

"What are we forgiving her for? For leaving us?" Loa looked up.

Marren nodded with a grunt. "It looks like we aren't getting inside, Petal. They aren't going to have time. You've been strong and patient, so how about we visit the store tomorrow?"

Loa nodded, swallowing to think it would be another year, before they could ask about Henya… and she couldn't help noticing her father's defeated stoop as they retreated back down the road to Homefields, the concentric rings of dome shaped homes in the crater basin, which surrounded the Breach Pit.

Glancing back up the hill she could see a great mob around the company store, and she thought how silly it was to buy something now, with everyone trying to spend their tokens at once.

"Do you think someone will buy the Gevrider today?"

Marren shook his head. "No one has that many tokens; I think it's just there for show."

Chapter 2

"SKITTERS!" a boy cried.

They were almost home, searching for a small brownstone dome in a forest of similar hovels. Loa could always spot their house by the white box that sat outside the door—it was an empty foam crate she often played with and used for putting things in. Because of the drill dust she couldn't bring it in the house, but she loved glimpsing it from afar, gleaming against the outer wall like a brilliant block of rock salt in a sea of faded bark rinds. Even better than the box was the fact that Derig wanted to see her, though she wasn't overly fond of the nickname. Her friends had once hijacked a tasking cart after curfew to go exploring, but gave away Loa's spot after she paid them two Glow-Ups for the privilege. Keia called her sad kitten for crying as they left... and soon sad-kitten had become 'Skitten' and then finally Skitters; but Loa really didn't mind so much. Derig was four years older than she, and Keia was even older, so Loa was always looking for things to tell them, or share with them. Derig was also taller and his shaved black hair was so short it looked almost painted on. Before Henya was sent underground Derig and Keia had been her friends too, and would have followed her anywhere.

Loa waved and smiled as she approached. Derig huffed up to her side as Marren left them and ducked into the house.

"What's on! Hey Skitters," Derig panted. "You guys get some tokens?"

"Yep," Loa beamed, pulling the round coppery coin from her pocket.

"I got four," Derig replied, tugging them from a pouch at his side.

"Wow," Loa said, hiding her disappointment.

"Plus my dad got four, plus Mirda got three, plus Alam got four. Plus Keia got four, and I don't know how many her mom and dad got. My mom didn't go she's still sick. But we could have had four more if she was there."

"Want to play pack up?" Loa asked, turning over the box. She knew it was a longshot but pretending to pack for a trip or a mission was always fun. Bits of rock or debris could be substituted for important items they were missing, or even for imaginary items they made up on the spot, like the laser scouter (a small flat rock) that Loa could hold up to her eye and use to spot any vapor sink or gas burn they might encounter. It was so powerful that she only had to check once, to predict every obstacle for the journey, and be sure of no accidents.

But Derig shrugged. "Dad bought pierolls, I think I'm just gonna go eat. Hey if you have any pierolls come over and bring some! We could always use more."

Loa crouched by her box and looked up at him. "I don't think we have any..." But she couldn't wait any more. "Also Derig, I have a secret. There's something I found, I want to show Keia too."

"What is it?"

"It's... it's a secret. It's really interesting. It's a secret place and I want to show—"

"Tell me about it later, I gotta go." He dashed off without another word as she placed a small square of debris in the box. Probably a communicator; she could use it if she got turned around in a dust wall on the trip. "Bye!" She yelled after him.

After packing a few more items she plopped onto the ground beside her box. It had been nearly a year since her best friend Ondi's family had been transferred to Gevroh Tharsis. Of the three mining planets in the Gevroh Corporation: Prime, Sekris, and Tharsis, Tharsis was the worst. Ondi had been a lot of fun; even smaller than Loa, but a little older. He fancied himself an inventor, and was actually good at it. Able to come up with some amazing contraptions, like a thing he called 'glodio' that would make a wire bend and light up when there were tunnels under your feet. Ondi had always been up for an adventure, and Loa missed him.

"Loa get in here and eat something. Dust is coming up it's time to get inside." Her father's voice sounded weak and fuzzy through the brownstone walls. Snatching the communicator from the junk in her box Loa kicked the dirt from her shoes and went in. The hovel was one large room with her little hanging loft near the peak of the ceiling. She adjusted the burwood boxes they used for chairs and sat down.

"Do we have any pierolls?"

Marren rounded his shoulders as he cut knots of barkroll from the rocky loaf onto plastin plates. "No, Loa. Derig has a large family, they get more company store and more rations."

"I know." She nodded. "I found this." She held up her communicator.

"That's a beam cap, makes them safer to move."

"Well, it's a communicator," she replied.

"So it is! Gloves off the table." He set the plate in front of her and added a few slices of rubeet, tipping them from a wide bowl. They weren't smoked, which might add a little more flavor, but fire was expensive. Loa kicked her feet as she made bites out of one slice of beet on top of each knuckle of barkroll. Together they were almost tasteless, though not as bad as they were separately.

"Pass the rock salt," Loa squeaked, and her father laughed. It was her joke at every meal; rock salt was something she'd never even tasted. At ten tokens for a small can, the seasoning was too pricey, and she knew only the most wasteful colonists would buy it.

Marren squeezed some rusty water into his mouth from the drink-skin that hung on a system of straps over their heads, and passed it to Loa. She sucked on the nozzle for a moment before coughing and pushing it away.

"I think I'm getting another Glow-Up tomorrow. Then I'll have four."

"That sounds nice, Petal... but I'm afraid they've changed the prices again. It's more expensive now."

Loa's stomach twisted. "Ok. I'll just get something else. "

"I'm sorry Loa, I'd give you another one, but I'm saving for that pair of steam goggles; mine are cracked."

"I know. I have three Glow-Ups still, I'm ok." She tried to smile but he reached across and took her hand.

"They won't need me at the drills tomorrow," he said. "It will be safe for you to go exploring with Keia and Derig again, if you want."

It was definitely something. Tomorrow would be the day. And once they saw it, things would be different. They would have to believe her, and she wouldn't need to be Skitters anymore.

Chapter 3

The next morning's trip to the company store was not as much fun as she'd hoped. As it turned out the entire price list had been adjusted, and a disappointed crowd stood murmuring in front of it as she struggled to see the changes. Liquings which had been one token were now three, and Glow-Ups were two. The Gel Figs had gone from five tokens to ten. Loa's face burned as she read the list, there was not a single item on it for one coin; everything was two or more.

Her father gave her a sheepish smile and patted her back when she emerged, squeezing against the dense current of shoppers until she popped out on the other side.

"We'll earn more soon, Petal, you'll see."

By the time afternoon began to wane her efforts to find Derig or Keia had proven fruitless, and so she decided to draw an elaborate map in the cracked dirt behind the house. It was slow going until she found a little metal gearwing with a spoke sticking out, which turned out to be perfect for cutting into the dry ground. She used dark pieces of debris and small rocks to mark important locations, and soon had come up with an impressive road map to the gray valley behind Homefields, with a pleasingly accurate miniature of the crash site and the ruptured earth hiding the secret place she'd found below it.

She was just kneeling to add a bauble to the wreckage of the cargo hulk, which needed another engine, when a pair of shiny new hauler boots landed in the middle of her map—splashing dirt and carefully placed landmarks all over her.

"Derig!" she spluttered, rubbing her eyes and spitting. The boy attached to the boots laughed.

"Did I mess up your city planning? Check on the boots! Twenty-five tokens, brand new." He turned them to the sides so she could see the Gevroh Corporation logo in brilliant red.

"You didn't have to do that." She pushed him off the remains of her map with a small sob.

"I know! But I wanted them... last year we gave the tokens to Alam, and Mirda already had boots so it was my turn. You can walk for days in these!"

"No, you broke my map, you didn't have to." She wanted to tell her father, but she snatched up the gearwing instead.

"Forget about the map Loa." Derig put his hand on her shoulder. "You've got the place inside your head right?"

"Yes." She glared at the boots.

"I told Keia about your secret, she wants to see it too, also my brother is coming and the Barris twins."

"Really? And Keia is coming?" Loa smiled in spite of herself.

"S'right. It better be interesting. Also Keia wanted me to ask if you have any Glow-Ups left. If you have one for her she'll definitely come. They're expensive now!"

"I do! I have three left." Loa fidgeted with the gearwing, wishing she'd been less specific.

"Wow! Can you get me one? I won't tell. Get me one right now before they get here."

"Oh… ok!" Loa dropped the tool and ran back around to the front of the house.

Moments later she had returned with the candy, a small sphere of deliciousness in dark purple wrapping perched on a white stick. The pulsing glow of the candy center could be seen through the wrapper, even in artificial daylight. Derig snatched it as soon as he could reach and tore it open with relish. Loa swallowed as he stuck the whole thing in his mouth, cupping his hands around his face to see the glow.

"Purple... Grapevine," He said through candy stuffed lips. He gave her a thumbs-up and spun around, finishing off the map with a few well-placed stomps. But Loa didn't care; her friends were coming over, and she was going to show them something amazing.

She'd hoped to be off as soon as Keia arrived, but it took a minute to stuff her little pack with a thick rag just in case someone needed to rest their head, and the beam cap communicator, and two slices of dried rubeet and a soft round pod of rusty water. Leaving the last Glow-Up for herself didn't work out, as Derig's older brother Alam asked if there were extra, and after taking the other Keia ordered Loa to get him the last one. Without any more candy to give away there was no reason to further delay the trip, and Loa began to feel quite cheerful again as she lead the way, authentic mining pole in hand, through the crowded lanes of Homefields and down the road. Soon they'd trekked out of the crater and into the open valley beyond, where if you walked far enough you'd come to much older abandoned mines, where the Gevroh Corporation had given up on finding whatever it was they were looking for. The terrain was rocky and course, broken by twisted trunks of enormous burwood trees—some of them towering near a hundred feet above the dusty ground, their ponderous canopies interlocking to scramble the artificial twilight, making networks of bright speckles on the valley floor around them. The Barris twins, both girls with shock platinum hair tied behind their heads, giggled and tittered at each other while Alam and Derig used their best show-off voices to tell stories of stealing tools after curfew and free-riding tasking carts. Keia was too important to laugh with them, being the oldest girl, and so Loa was able to chat with her excitedly; though the teenage Keia responded rarely and only paused between yawns to check their progress. She was as tall as Alam, with straight sandy hair and sleepy eyes.

"Are you sure this is right?"

"Oh yes," Loa replied. "And we're allowed to see the wreck anyway, but the bottom of it is underground."

"The wreck isn't new Loa. Are we supposed to crawl under it?"

"Sort of—not really. We'll go inside it first. It's really big down there."

"Is that the secret?" Keia asked with a sucking noise, still rolling the Glow-Up stick around in her teeth. Bananade was a good flavor, but not the best.

"No, I mean, that's where we go to it," Loa said. "But the secret is something there." The excitement began to rise in her throat as she spoke.

"You know we don't have much time right? We've got two hours before night bell."

"That's ok, it's really interesting. We have enough time."

Keia rolled her eyes and shrugged, and the group resigned to follow their guide a while longer...

Chapter 4

Being the smallest, Loa had no trouble squeezing inside once they found the right spot. The cargo hulk was truly immense, over a hundred feet long and half as tall, with fat round wings buried in the dirt. The Corporation had long ago decided unearthing the wreckage was not cost effective, and for nearly ten years the shell of the hulk had been a favorite destination for colony youngsters. Once while exploring by herself, which was how it usually worked out, Loa had discovered a pocket of cold air beneath one arm of the hulk's forward loader. After that it was a simple matter of digging. Now, with her friends behind her she stood proudly on the open deck of the ship itself, some twenty feet below the valley floor outside, with only a crack of light coming from the place where she had broken through. After much scrambling and complaining the others managed to climb inside and join her, looking sulky and annoyed as they smacked and brushed the dirt from each other. Loa nodded happily and twisted the silver tip of the wandlight she'd packed, pointing the light deeper into the ship.

"The stairs there takes us to the fuel door on the bottom, and the door is stuck open, and that's where I found it."

"Loa, come Tasking Day you better believe you're helping us out." Keia was angry. "This better be really cool." Tasking Days were the only time children could earn tokens on their own, and Loa found Keia and her friends were more likely to play with her if she let them help spend what she earned.

"Follow me!" she chirped and clanked off in her worn dustboots to the stairs. Descending was not difficult, though with the entire ship at a strange angle it made Loa a little dizzy. Moments later they had all banged to the bottom and stood around a wide open hatch that led down into darkness.

"The bottom is really close," Loa said as she drew circles with the wandlight. Indeed the bottom of the hole could not have been more than eight feet below, though it was strangely cracked and sunken, as though it might fall a moment later into whatever was beneath.

"There's a tunnel," Loa continued. "It's small but if you lie down at the top and peak down there you can see a light, and it's really far away... it's far away and it's straight down. But you can't see it yet you have to crawl to the edge."

Keia crossed her arms. "That doesn't make any sense, Loa. There's nothing down there, we're standing on solid rock."

"Just come in here and look for a second." Loa was already climbing carefully around the lip of the door, grabbing at the clamps that lined the near wall of the fuel chamber and using them like a ladder. She landed on the bottom and looked up expectantly.

"Come down and see! I'm going to turn off the light and then we can see it and we can hopefully also hear it."

"Hear it?!" One of the Barris twins suddenly yelped and began to whimper.

Alam laughed. "Scared? Scared little kitten? Look at Skitters—she's not scared now is she? Move." Shoving Keia out of the way as she leaned over the opening, Alam jumped in, landing beside Loa and helping her sneeze on a cloud of dust.

Derig gaped after him but remained rooted in place.

"Now what?" Alam looked down at their guide and tapped the crack with his foot.

"No, that's solid. It's down here." Loa dropped to her knees and scuttled into the dark wedge between the wall of the ship and the ground. "The crack gets big here."

Alam struggled after her.

"Be careful you idiots!" Keia yelled. "All we can see is your boots."

"Now…" Loa clicked off the wandlight to peak over the edge where the crack split and became wider. Alam poked his head over beside hers. At first there was nothing but absolute blackness and a cold draught that slipped past their faces with a smell of damp earth, but then a flicker, like a far off light in a hazy dream, winked up at them out of the black.

"By the beating Core how far down is that?!" Alam gasped.

"I told you it was interesting!" Loa could barely contain herself. She had enjoyed imagining her friends here with her and had never really thought they would come, and while she would rather have shown the strange light to Keia, it was still good to share it with Alam. He hadn't even eaten his Glow-Up yet. It was Cherryboom, her favorite.

After a few minutes of whispering and some complaining from Derig and Keia they heard it—a distant scrape, like the noise made by something dragged across a hollow metal surface. The sound bounced up the dark shaft and into their ears several more times before melting away. Alam was gasping and laughing.

"So amazing! We should climb closer! Can you climb down a bit? Can you fit in there?"

"Ok! I think..." Loa clenched her fists and swelled with pride as she twisted around to put her legs in first. Everyone would be waiting to see if she could do it. The tunnel was not quite straight down, and was narrow and textured enough for her to hold on... a little closer and she could tell them more about what was down there. Alam was clambering back out from under the fuel hatch when she clicked the wandlight on again. Alam shouted at the others.

"It's a tunnel and there was a light! It's real! She's going down there, it's fantastic! This is the most amazing thing ever, you guys have to come down here."

"No! We're staying up here thanks," Keia yelled, her voice shaking. "This is really stupid. There's nothing here—all she found is a hole that shouldn't be there. So what. We can't be out here so late—" A sudden squeal cut through the air, and Keia's mouth closed with a snap. Loa had slipped.

Chapter 5

She slid for what felt like minutes before coming to rest in a slight bend, wedged in the tunnel. The wandlight bounced free and clattered down into darkness, on and on until with a faint tinkling it hit the bottom. Her knee was jammed into one corner with her pants torn through, the skin scraped raw and burning. Looking up Loa could see a frantic beam of light searching the walls and hear them calling, but her voice was caught in her throat as her vision wobbled with tears. Her hands and feet began to tingle with a frozen panic.

"Loa!" The shouts were far away but came clearer when the speaker put his face near the mouth of the tunnel. She could hear Keia and Alam arguing.

"Look what you made her do! My parents will kill me!" Keia was shrieking as Alam yelled at her.

"We don't know what happened she could be ok down there! We have to get help!"

"I'm not here! I can't be here this never happened! We're leaving!"

"Wait!" But Loa's own voice was little more than a whisper. The tears streamed into her mouth as she scrabbled at the walls and tried to straighten her leg. She wanted to yell but the sound wouldn't come; replaced instead with a choking sob as clods of rocky dirt broke free in her hands. After a few more moments of fruitless clawing she strained to hear the voices again, but they were gone.

And then it happened. Part of the tunnel wall shifted, and she was tumbling, falling. Her fingers bounced against the sides as she tried to slow her descent, but it was no use. The sound of sliding dirt and bounding rocks pressed in as the darkness tumbled with her. At last she broke free and careened through cold empty air into the chamber below—colliding with the stone floor in a splash of hands and knees; her head hitting last, softened by the pack that slipped underneath her. All sound stretched into a thin high pitched chord, her eyelids flickered, and she was out.

It might have been hours, or even longer, before she awoke. She felt groggy, hungry and thirsty, and her forehead still smarted, though her knees and wrists seemed better. No sooner had she sat up, but the terror of her situation came scrambling back. The dark was absolute, and the silence gave every breath an echo. As she tried to look around, her eyes working on a fresh batch of tears, she put her hand on the lost wandlight, and immediately snatched it up.

The little beam spread and revealed the room was vast, with a flat carved ceiling and dark empty walls. Behind her was the outline of what looked to be a large stone door—nearly invisible in the smooth surrounding wall. Turning her light across the colorless flagstones of the floor she paused at a large object on the other end of the room. It was an enormous chair, and someone was sitting in it. It looked to be a dark, faceless person, with bowed head and wearing deep black, very tall even sitting—surely much bigger than any regular adult. Unsure whether to shine the light or turn it off Loa stood shaking, making fists in her shirt as new tears followed the familiar path to her chin. But the figure did not move. Blinking through the wetness she noticed a small glimmering something sitting in its lap—it looked almost like an old fashioned wristwatch from where she stood. Too afraid to approach, or to move away, or to speak, she merely stood and pointed the wandlight, and waited. She knew the little light was good for years, but eventually the thought of actually being stuck here that long roused her into taking a step forward. And another.

There was her pack. She sat slowly, grabbing it to snap it open. Her mouth was dry, but the water pod had burst, so it was all gone. She tried a bite of rubeet, but it was too tough, and she spit it out. The rag at least was still there, folded and soft. But what use was that now?

She stood up, thinking there was nothing to do, but go closer to the giant chair, and have a look. Slowly she crept closer, and after many quivering paces she could just see its face, yet still it had none. Or rather the figure's face was covered entirely in a sort of fitted black material, like a special sock made for someone's head. Its body was humanlike though quite imposing, with broad shoulders and four fingers with a thumb resting on each knee. She could hear no sound of breath nor see it move, though her heart jumped when the light danced off the object in its lap. A hinged bracelet of tarnished golden metal with a deep red stone set in the outside—it looked small and strangely out of place in the figure's lap, though it sparkled with enough dust and moisture to have been there quite some time. And then, for no reason she could think of, she reached out to touch it. The figure's leg was hard and cool, as though someone had dressed a statue all in black. Breathing quickly she touched the hand. Still cold, like stone. She reached toward the bracelet and froze—there was the sound, the same sound she had heard from so far above, but this time it was all around her. The figure's chest swelled and its head tilted back as a great scraping noise filled the room. Loa fell to the ground and muffled a squeal, curling into a ball with the wandlight switched off. The scraping subsided, and she understood. It was breathing. The wandlight flicked on again, but the figure had not moved. Her lips cracked as her tiny voice struggled to return.

"Hello?" It was the faintest whisper, but echoed in the stillness. The figure did not react.

Using the rag for a blanket, Loa sat on the cold floor in the center of the room, holding her knees with her face buried in her arms. She thought of her father, of their little house, of her white box outside and how she could swing on the hanging ladder that dangled from her loft. The loft was only for her... it was the coziest place she knew, with room for her bed and a little shelf with a bin for various important things like her Glow-Ups, when she had some. Grapevine, Bananade, Applecorp, Cherryboom… and Villymint, which she tried and didn't like. She'd only gotten to enjoy the apple. But it was stupid to think of candy now. Henya would be braver, if it was her stuck down here.

Loa bit her lip hard, hard enough to hurt more than the little knot on her forehead, and she was just thinking of that, and how hungry she was, when something cold touched her leg, and she shrieked. The beam of wandlight danced wildly as she scrambled to her feet to search the room. The figure was still in its chair, unmoved. But something was different. Looking again at the floor she saw the bracelet; up on one side and rocking slightly. It had rolled right into her leg where she sat.

She ran to the other side, and after a few desperate minutes finding out the seamless looking door really was just like a wall, she shuffled back to her spot and sat down by the bracelet. Leaning over and nearly touching it with the wandlight, she shined the beam on every surface. The metal looked as though it had once been brilliant gold but was so faded now that it was almost gray; the band must have been an inch wide, with not one but three small dark red stones on the outside. There were all sorts of etchings on it, complex patterns and lines at right angles, but nothing that looked like letters. Loa shivered, huddling in closer to study the object, and she noticed that the gold markings would glow for a few moments even with the wandlight off; as though they were capturing some its light, and reluctant to let it go.

There was nothing left but to touch it. She picked it up and opened the hinge. The thing was as cold as it looked, and the stones shone dark red in the refracted light. Checking the figure one more time she fastened the bracelet on her wrist with a frown and stared at it. Oddly enough it fit just right. She wiped her eyes with her forearm, and rubbed a finger over the markings.

The figure stood up. Stifling a gasp Loa dragged herself backward until she could stand and wedge into the far corner. She turned the wandlight off then back on again. Like a shadow's shadow the figure walked toward her, making not a sound. It must have been at least seven feet tall and loomed ever larger as it approached. Loa shrank down and held up her hands, her heart pounding in her throat. The figure stopped in front of her and she closed her eyes, huffing and spluttering as she covered her head.

She waited, trembling. Nothing happened. She looked up. The figure was close enough to step on her but only stood there, looking down. She could hear the rasping metal breath, though it was much quieter now.

Moments passed. It didn't move, and neither did she, until finally the dread couldn't get any bigger, and she'd had enough.

"Help!" She yelled suddenly, and covered her head again. The figure raised its arm, reaching for the door. The stone moved as though in response, and the immensity of the door melted away, revealing the tallest flight of stairs Loa had ever seen.

Chapter 6

Halfway up her stomach panged and growled, and weak with hunger she had to stop, and promptly fell asleep. She woke after some while, and found the second half of the climb easier, partly from excitement to reach the expanding light at the top. Her feet ached and her legs burned, but at last she tumbled out of a narrow crack in the rocky wall of the valley, and rolled a good ways through all manner of unpleasant underbrush, until she came to rest in a patch of brown curl-grass, within shouting distance of the crash site. The projected sun high in the sky told her it was late afternoon. Heart hammering, she scampered through the dust to the rounded wing of the cargo hulk, and leaning against it she managed a few tired cries but heard nothing back. Clearly her friends had gone home, or to look for help. A sudden blast of sound from the sky made her jump. Looking up she saw a low flying capital ship with telltale bright red hull and glimmering silver trim—the Gcvroh Corporation overseers were returning.

She burst through the front door with a shout, and her father looked up, his face pale with shock. He was sitting at the table, upon which were two square gray cases.

"Loa?" his voice cracked.

"Dad!" she panted. "You'll never believe it, we went to the—"

But in two steps her father had crossed the room, and grabbed her.

His embrace squashed the breath out of her, but Loa hugged him back as hard as she could, clenching her eyes.

"I'm hungry!"

Marren laughed as he set her down. "You're in trouble young lady," he said, though there was relief in his voice. "But first, let's eat."

"What are these?" she asked, pulling up a box to sit.

"EMKs," he said. "It was three days Loa… three days. They came to tell me the search was called off, and this is what they gave me, instead of finding…" he nodded, choking up.

"Three days?" Loa stared at him. "No, it couldn't be…"

Marren cleared his throat. "Three days," he repeated, and sliding one of the boxes to her he cracked it open.

She knew EMK stood for Enforce Meal Kit, but she'd never seen one up close. Only the Gevroh company people could have them. Looking inside the case her stomach did a flip. There was a jar of fresh juice, and a tube of vegetable protein beside the main dish. There was even a quart pouch of clear water. She wanted to drink but the protein tube was already in her mouth, and she sucked down the green protein with a growl, not caring if it was rubeet. But it wasn't, it was something else, something wonderful. Her father stood over her, he peeled open the bowl, and the smell of cooked potato with shredded meat in broth almost knocked her out. Carefully unwrapping the enclosed utensil, she took her first bite, and shivered. It was more flavor than she thought a mouth could taste, and there was a sharp extra something in every morsel… rock salt, it had to be.

Her father opened his own case, and joined her in the feast. Loa stopped for a drink between bites, and found the water was pure and cool, it didn't taste like rust at all. Too busy for talking, they worked their way through the stew, and under the napkin, in its own little pocket Loa discovered a puffy Gel Fig. She considered waiting, but before she knew it the treat was unwrapped and in her mouth, where it melted to thick powdery goodness; it tasted just like the color pink.

"This is FOOD!" Loa said thickly, making just enough air in her mouth to talk, before washing it down with juice.

Marren's eyes were wet. "These kits are special," he said, "only Enforcers who work inside the complex can get them."

"Why?"

"I don't know. But that's where detention and reeducation is; perhaps yelling at children is hard work."

Loa giggled at this, reminded that sometimes that seemed to be true, when she misbehaved.

But her father wasn't smiling, he looked more tired than he ever had. "Petal, I know you like to explore, but you have to promise me, you will never do that again."

"I'm sorry," she said, slumping in her chair with a full belly. "Was I really gone three days? I can't believe it."

"Yes," her father said, watching as she guzzled the last of her juice.

"One of your friends left me a note, all it said was you fell in a hole… in the valley."

"That's not true," she said, wiping her mouth. "Well… kind of." But the words were jumbled, as a woozy craving for sleep rushed in to take hunger's place. She wanted to tell him everything, about the tunnel, and the statue that moved, and the stairs up through the ground… but more than that she wanted to climb the swinging ladder to her loft, and make sure her bed was there, just as she left it.

"Can I go to sleep?"

"Of course, Petal, we'll talk later."

Up in her little space, there was a round mattress and pillow, with Wolby the cotton man, whom her mother had sewn and filled with downy fluff from an old work vest. And there was a shelf with four tiny bristle people, which Loa had made by twisting scraper fibers together, beside her little candy bin, now empty. Unrolling the blanket she snuggled in, closing her eyes. As she drifted off she felt her wrist, just to touch it again… she could show her father the bracelet tomorrow.

But she jerked awake; the bracelet was gone. Instead she found a gray band of skin around her wrist, as though the bracelet had somehow stained her arm before slipping off. Too drowsy to puzzle over it now, she scratched her arm a few moments, and rolled over to sleep.

The part of her dream that she could remember began with a trip to the company store, where she was given a beautiful Blueblare Glow-Up for free, but it suddenly grew so large that she couldn't lift it. Moments later she found herself looking over the highest edge of the crater into the dark of Homefields far below, where only a single light flickered in the silent sea of deserted hovels. She was holding her father's hand but when she looked up his face was covered in shadow.

"That's our house," she said, pointing at the single glowing light.

"Thank you Loa," her father's voice was strange, deep and distant as though he was speaking from the end of a long tunnel.

"For what?" She noticed there were lines of golden light dancing under the skin of his hand, moving at right angles to disappear up the darkness of his arm.

"For coming to find me," he replied.

Loa looked up. "You're not my dad, are you."

"No. You're dreaming, Petal. Wake up."

She pondered the dream and her time under the crash site often over the next few days, and though at first no excuse was too small to talk about what happened, she soon grew weary and frustrated that no one cared to believe her. She wanted desperately to know where the bracelet had gone, and it was no small nuisance that the gray band on her wrist proved impervious to even the most aggressive scrubbing. But without the bracelet, or any other evidence, her friends decided teasing was the best response; especially when it came to the part about a tall shadowy figure, like a statue, that had saved her life. On the other hand she found the idea that she'd been missing for three whole days just as ridiculous. Derig's brother Alam was the only one in the group who didn't make fun of her, and he agreed the mark on her wrist must be proof of *something* mysterious. He even apologized for taking her last Glow-Up, though the others only laughed.

Marren was an easier audience, grateful as he was to have her back, but his lack of faith in the dark figure was disappointing. And when a small expedition lead by Loa herself failed to turn up the doorway she had rolled out of, or the staircase leading down to the room with the throne, she was forced to take the humiliation and admit defeat. Even Alam seemed less curious after running his hand over the 'doorway' and finding solid rock. Along with these disappointments came another even sharper; now that the Imperial fleet had left, lots more Corporation soldiers and overseers descended on Lantus Crater, while broadcasts barked about woeful reductions in efficiency, threatening that *commensurate punishment* was forthcoming. Loa had also failed to show up on her last Tasking Day, which meant she would work the following week for one token instead of a chance for three, and probably be assigned a more dangerous job. Her father, who had been on a committee to review labor abuses for the Imperial overseers, was now under observation, and he told a disappointed Loa that trips to the store would have to be less frequent, even for window shopping. She was further distressed to learn that a pre-curfew alarm had been instituted, requiring all children under the age of thirteen to be inside well before the others.

"But it's not even dark!" She protested as her father lead her home by the wrist a few evenings later.

"The light isn't real, Loa, you know that—the dome is light or dark because their machines make it that way. We've got to follow the rules, so there's no more exploring—no more sneaking around, not now." He sounded distracted and impatient, and Loa huffed and growled as she plodded after him. She made a point by climbing emphatically up the swinging ladder instead of having dinner, though a growling stomach made her regret it, and not for the first time she wished they'd saved something from the EMKs. Barkrolls and rubeet had even less flavor now than before.

The following morning seemed impossibly early, until she realized it was still the middle of the night.

"Loa! Loa I need you to wake up. There's no one to watch you right now, I need you to come with me." Her father sounded excited, and judging by the scuffling paper sounds beneath her he was in a rush to gather his journals.

"I don't need a minder." She rolled to the edge and peaked down at him.

"I want you in my sight. We're going to community hall and it has to be right now."

Chapter 7

The community hall meeting was clearly a secret; attended by a few dozen darkly clad men and women who shuffled to their seats as they entered, arranging themselves in a hushed circle around the dim light of a single emerald electorch planted on the floor in the center. Marren lead Loa by the hand to a spot near the door and told her to sit on the floor quietly behind him, as there were not enough chairs. A small hairless man wearing a heavy smock and dark mining goggles walked to the torch and held up his arms for silence.

"I have been in communication with Liaison Udira, and our guess was right. The Imperials will not be returning." His voice was soft but carried over the muttering crowd. "At this point Marren's operation is the only way forward, and I believe he has brought the plans. We will need a full scale catastrophe to provoke the next intervention."

There were a few gasps and more muttering.

A hooded woman stood up suddenly. "Fogus, if we stop the drills, the Corporation will have our homes long before the Imperial Sanctor hears anything. Sabotage gets them their way even faster—we can't give them a better excuse to destroy our families!"

"Darta listen," said Fogus, the man in the center. "Like every corp under the grace of the Imperium, Gevroh is answerable to its employer—the yield from Lantus Crater funnels directly into the Toron column; it's a vital part of the largest resource vein in this sector. Cutting off our contribution, even for a moment, will get us the attention we need."

"And the children?" Another man had stood up, with short oily hair and a long mustache. "How many of us have sons or daughters in detention? If this goes wrong it's not us who get punished—it's the little ones. Like my son Tuke here," he gestured at a small boy standing behind him. "Barely large enough to handle a motepick, he wouldn't make it down there."

Loa startled as her father stood up in front of her.

"You all know I have a child in detention," Marren said. "Henya has been down there two years." He looked around the room before continuing. "And you know the Corporation's safety standards took my wife." There was some murmuring of ascent. "My youngest, Loa, is here with us tonight." He reached down and Loa stood up quickly, taking his hand.

"Good to have you back Loa," someone said. "You're a very lucky child!"

Marren moved her to stand in front of him, presenting her to the group. "The Corporation put the value of her life at two EMKs," he said. "I thank the Core, to have her back. But we can't go on like this. We have to act…"

Loa looked down, trying to be smaller. She studied the tiny holes in the tops of her boots, and the wires breaking away where the soles met the treads. The gray dustboots had been brown when they were new; they belonged to Henya when she was Loa's age. Marren squeezed her shoulders, clearing his throat.

"Friends, we have the power, in this room, to make them listen. The Corporation's Enforcers haven't come back to bore us with efficiency charts. Their supervisors are gone, and now they want revenge. If the Empire won't help, we have to do it ourselves."

A heavy man with beady eyes squished into the wrinkles of his face stood up. "My son is in detention; I'm with Marren. We can't rely on the Empire for help—not unless we make them notice us again. The reds will go back to throwing young ones in the hole for the slightest offense. We need a spark. I call a vote."

Everyone started talking at once, and Marren sat back down in his chair, slumping over. Loa stood behind his chair again, and she mustered a smile for Tuke, who was across from her, but he didn't seem to notice. He looked as sleepy as she was.

The man at the center held his hands up and spoke. "I need a show of hands. Everyone please—quiet." The shifting and chattering tapered off, and Marren raised his hand. A few others followed quickly, and then most of them had a hand up.

"Do I raise my hand?" Loa leaned to ask.

"No, Petal, just listen, the meeting is almost over."

The man in the goggles seemed satisfied. "That's it then. We'll call our little mutiny official; sabotage of the drills will begin." He smiled strangely, and fidgeted with an inner pocket of his smock before continuing. "Unfortunately,

I am afraid this is as far as we get. The Corporation must find you guilty one and all, of conspiracy."

Everyone seemed to stiffen. "Fogus, what is this?" Marren demanded. "What are you doing?"

"I'm sorry Marren, but Lantus Crater is a speck of rust in a rainstorm; it was never going to happen."

Most of the adults jumped to their feet, and Loa felt a familiar knot forming in her stomach. Something was very wrong. One of the men made to rush at Fogus but he withdrew his hand from his smock and there was a blinding flash. A crushing press of white hot air splashed into Loa's face and it felt as though invisible fingers were closing in, shutting down her senses. She collapsed to the floor, slipping into unconsciousness as the shouting grew distant, punctuated at last by the sound of the community hall doors breaking down.

Loa woke with a grunt and found she was sitting in an armchair. It was deep and soft, facing an imposing black desk that curved away from her on either side to frame a large high-backed chair. As she blinked the drowsiness from her eyes and tried to remember what had happened she saw the entire wall beyond the desk was window; dark and smoky with various charts and monitor screens trapped in the glass. Outside she could see the Breach Pit far below, with the great arms of the Master Drill rising and falling like the legs of an enormous insect stuck on its back.

No sooner had she discovered that she was strapped to the chair than she noticed the wrist with the gray mark was itchy and sore, with needle-point marks and scrapes. She wanted to rub and scratch it, but twisting against the straps was no use.

"Easy dear," It was a woman's voice behind her, one she had never heard. "We have a few questions for you, and you'll be back home before you know it. My name is Aridonna Gevroh, and I'm very pleased to finally meet you."

The woman walked around to the high-backed chair, dropping a small silver datapad on the desk's glossy surface before taking a seat. She was older than Loa's father, with silver hair in a wide plait over her shoulder, and a dark red Gevroh Corporation suit that clasped at the front of her throat with a small green dot. Loa looked around the office and shook against the binding straps. The room was dark and mostly red, with a huge monitor on one side and the Gevroh Corporation logo on the other.

"Let me off here!" She tried her best for angry rather than scared, but the way Aridonna Gevroh smiled made her lip tremble. A door opened behind them and heavy boots entered the room. The woman raised her eyebrows expectantly.

"Well?" Her voice was harsh. A man wearing a bulky Corporate Enforcer uniform, complete with larger version of the visored helmet available at the company store, stepped to the woman's side and leaned in to speak.

"Every test inconclusive, but it's definitely something. There's no sign of the device."

"So take the arm," Aridonna hissed through the side of her mouth.

"Now?" The man replied.

"Not now you imbecile, after we're finished here." The man nodded and strode from the room, sliding the door shut behind him.

"I apologize for that!" Aridonna crooned. "Please stop squirming Loa, I only have a few questions, and then you can go, and we will pay you for your time."

"I want to go home," Loa stopped rocking against the chair and glared. The knot in her stomach was tightening. "I didn't do anything. My dad didn't do anything. Where is he?"

"He's safe in our care, only for a little while," Aridonna continued. "Now—let's get this done shall we? And then you will be off home, with a little present." She pulled a small box out from under the desk and set it on top, rubbing her finger along the hinge. The box sprang open and Loa could see stacks of gleaming tokens inside.

"I need to ask you dear, about the tomb."

Still trembling, but keeping her eyes on the tokens Loa clenched her hands and nodded. "The what?"

"The tomb dear—the tomb you stumbled into. Deep underground. The company has been looking for it for a very long time. And you found it first! You are a very lucky little girl."

"Isn't tomb where they bury someone?"

"Yes dear, that's the place."

"Then it wasn't a tomb. Just a very tall man in black, sitting on a chair like a throne; and he wasn't dead. Well, he wasn't a person I guess."

Aridonna stared at her with narrowing eyes. "You saw this figure walking? Moving?"

"Yes, I didn't know what he wanted and he never talked, but then he let me out of there. He made a stairs and it went right out to the top."

"Did you take something from the tomb Loa? Something that didn't belong to you?"

Loa's face burned. "There was a bracelet, it had strange designs, and I only put it on for a minute... but I lost it."

"You lost it?" The woman's voice rose. "Where did you lose it?"

"I don't know where it came off, or how that happened—it disappeared and my arm has this gray ring on it." This was clearly not the right answer, and the woman looked angry.

Tears welled in Loa's eyes. "I looked for the bracelet but I couldn't find it. And now my arm really hurts. I didn't mean to steal anything!"

"And you've been telling all your little friends about this haven't you? Why didn't you have your father send us a report? You really should have you know."

"I don't think he believed me. Not the part about the tall man... or the bracelet."

"That bracelet is very important, and I pray the mark on your arm isn't all that's left of it!" She seemed to be working to contain her frustration.

"What is the tomb for? Was someone really buried there?" Loa asked softly, trying to change the subject.

Aridonna clenched her jaw as she leaned back. The high-backed chair turned to the windows and she was hidden from view.

"Can I go now?" Loa pressed.

"What you found my dear, is the tomb of a Star Shadow, one of the oldest. There he has been hidden for hundreds of years."

"What's Star Shadow?" Loa couldn't help herself, but the woman only gestured with a snap and the door slid open. More boot steps and two men with large red gloves unlocked the straps over Loa's arms. The bindings popped open and they grabbed her, hoisting her over the back of the chair and forcing her to the door.

"Wait! I can still look for the bracelet! Where is my dad?" All thoughts of tokens and the company store were dashed as the men pulled her through the portal into a dark hallway.

"Take her down!" Aridonna's voice called as the door slid closed.

Chapter 8

The men moved too quickly for Loa to keep up, and so her toes dragged against the floor. Tears pooled in her eyes as their large hands clenched into her arms, pinching and hurting. The hall was dim, lit only by narrow strips of red light that raced along the ceiling as they marched. Steadily the path descended, and squirm as she might there was no way to slow them down.

"She said I could go home!"

A few hundred feet later a panel opened and she was tossed into a brightly lit chamber. The gray wall shut behind her, and the men were gone. After a few whimpers and some pounding she wiped her face with a frown, and looked around the room. There were glass cases filled with little metal and plastin implements along either side, and a large table in the center draped with a white blanket under a bank of monitors. On each side of the table were metal straps that curled upward like little arms, waiting to clamp down on whoever might lie there.

Her shoulders trembled as Loa pulled the scarf off her head and clenched it in her hands. A loud hiss made her start, and she watched as frothy white steam filled the room, spraying from the four corners of the ceiling. An aggressive dizziness came on, and she lost her balance. Dropping to her hands and knees she slumped over, and closed her eyes.

When she opened them the bright ceiling warmed into focus, spinning around a central light. She yelped and struggled, but the straps of the table held her firmly, with her right arm clamped down by her side, and her left braced so it stuck straight out.

"No!" She yelled at the top of her lungs. The light in the room dimmed for a moment. A spastic movement caught her eye and she strained to turn her head. There was a balding man in a heavy white uniform looking at the ceiling.

"Control! We don't need any creative power allocation, thank you. The prison field isn't the priority right now." His voice was creaky and dry. Another voice filled the room in response, it was Aridonna Gevroh.

"What are you babbling about? The prison field is nominal; the colonists are docile. My shuttle leaves in fifteen minutes. I want some very good news on my way out. Get to the procedure."

"Of course Madam Gevroh, I'll have the article packaged in moments." He turned to face Loa and smiled in a yellowish, cracked sort of way. His eyes were covered by a dark visor that glowed green in the center.

"You're a lively one; the mist should have had you asleep for another half hour at least."

"No!" Whatever was about to happen she knew she wanted none of it. The light overhead flickered again.

"Dammit Control! I don't care if the drills hit solid arcidite—leave my lab out of it!" The man spat as he yelled, turning to yank open one of the cases at the wall. "The grid has got to be 100 years old... and they want me to work like this," he muttered.

"Dr. Hauge, we're not re-allocating, those power fluctuations are isolated to your office." The response was laced with background static.

"Ridiculous." Dr. Hauge huffed, holding up a small needle filled with a glowing blue fluid.

"I want to go home!" Loa's breath came in short gasps as she fought against the table.

"In a moment you'll be feeling so good you won't care; we just need the arm." He looked up to tap a few buttons on a low hanging monitor.

The knot in Loa's stomach felt ready to burst. "NO!" She screamed at the top of her lungs, and with a shattering pop the lights went out.

The doctor pelted the air with curses as a bead of emergency track-light circled the room near the floor.

"Control, I'll have your heads for this!" he roared, opening a small pair of silver tongs connected by a glowing wire. Loa blinked to clear the tears from her eyes as she watched him, but there was a fuzzy shadow in her vision that wouldn't go away. Lifting her head as best she could she trembled uncontrollably as the doctor grabbed her arm below the wrist.

The shadow behind him grew suddenly larger, building to a very tall humanoid shape. The doctor turned with a shriek and gaped as the dark figure from the tomb stood just before him. With a flicker of movement it planted a kick in his stomach, knocking his feet out from under him as he crashed straight through the panel wall to land on his face in the hallway, sliding backward. The figure turned for the table and Loa clenched her hands against the shivering as she stared into the black featureless face. With a whine of mechanical protest the straps broke apart and twisted back like withered plants. She was free.

What happened next felt more like a dream than something real. A piercing alarm began to sound; prompting Loa to grab her ears and cringe, but when the figure offered its hand she took it at once, hopping down off the table and snatching her scarf off the floor to tie it back on her head. Turning to the wall the dark figure raised its arm and a section of the white clinical steel dissolved into smoke, leaving a gaping hole and a staircase climbing upwards. Still clutching the hand of her benefactor Loa climbed the stairs beside him, trying to catch her breath.

"Can you... talk?" She heard her own voice, but felt like someone else had dared ask the question.

The figure did not respond.

After climbing long enough for her legs to feel hot and weak they emerged into the night air of the valley. She turned to see the shifting hole was in the knotted trunk of an enormous burwood tree, and she could still see the doctor's office far below. The figure released Loa's hand and raised its arm, pointing up and to the east, in the direction of Homefields. Loa nodded, and she turned to scramble up the curl-grass covered dune out of the lower valley.

No sooner had she reached the top when she gave a cry and turned back.

"Wait!" The dark figure remained unmoving as she slid and stumbled back down the dust billowing slope to meet him. "Wait," she pleaded, stooping for a sneeze before stopping in front of him. "They took my dad. And lots of other people. Can you help me get my dad? His name is Marren, Marren Dantrue. I don't know where they took him! Please save him!" The air around the figure seemed to bend and darken, and it was gone.

Puzzled, Loa searched for the figure in vain, but she was too close to Homefields for yelling—on the off chance there was a patrol nearby, so she kicked the dust and climbed back up the hill for the long walk home.

Chapter 9

Her head nodded as she walked, but there was a burst of wakefulness when she saw their hovel was in shambles, the door broken open.

"Dad?"

Bungling through the debris she looked up to see her loft bed hanging by one side of the harness. The mattress was on the floor and her things were scattered; Wolby lay half torn open and her bin was crushed. Snatching him up with angry tears she tried to push the stuffing back into his legs. Her father's bed was thrown off its platform, and even Henya's little cot had been taken down off the wall and broken apart. Food cabinets had been smashed and rifled through. Bits of Marren's maps and papers were scattered everywhere, along with the odd scrap of clothing or melting lump of rubeet. Still clutching Wolby Loa grabbed her mattress and dragged it to a clear spot near her father's upturned desk before hopping out of her boots. She pulled a trampled blanket off the floor and curled herself beneath it, slipping into an exhausted slumber.

She could tell by the light in the air that it really was a dream this time. There was more than blackness and stars outside the Lantus Crater dome-shield; there was a beautiful golden sky, a real sky, with giant shapes whirling past, like impossibly large puffy blankets of smoke or mist, miles above the surface. Beyond the wall of the dome she could see hills and fields covered in something that looked like curl-grass but softer, and green. There was a towering city in the distance, dotted with glimmering spires and brilliant lights. The city stood in the open, without any sort of dome-shield to protect it. Something about the place made her smile, and she wanted to dash to the crater gate and get outside, to run in the grass and feel the golden light on her face.

"Loa," The voice was all around her, and behind her. It was hollow and familiar, with a deep resonance unlike any human voice she had ever heard. She turned to see the dark figure standing in front of her house, the door caved in, just as it was in the real world.

"Where are we?" Loa asked, rushing toward him.

"Sleeping," the figure answered. As she drew close she could see cracks of golden light pulsing up the figure's arms to vanish as they fanned out across his chest and neck.

"I wish I hadn't lost the bracelet," she said, feeling sad, and a little guilty. "I think they came home and smashed everything, looking for it."

The figure crouched, so the featureless face was level with hers. "You don't need the bracelet, Petal. I can hear you, wherever you are. Things are going to change, but I need your guidance. I am not yet free."

"I want my dad, and my sister," Loa said miserably, and looking down she saw the ambient light dimmed from gold to a faint glimmer of silver; it was night again in Lantus Crater. She felt real tears sliding down her cheeks, tickling her ears where they soaked into the mattress, but she couldn't wake up, not yet. "Will you help us?"

"Yes."

The figure's face was soft, indistinct as it faded into the shadows, but the voice was deep and clear, hanging in the air as she opened her eyes. There was quiet in the house, and *something* was missing, but Loa could not imagine what it was. She found Wolby by her foot and untangled herself from the blanket. Jumping up she ran to the door and out into the pale artificial daylight.

"Dad?!" She cried desperately, but saw no one. Straining to listen she found the wind machines that were normally quiet could now be heard quite plainly. She followed the mining road with her eyes as it circled the valley, rising higher and higher past the company store to the central Corporation complex on the ridge of the crater. There were plumes of black smoke belching from the Breach Pit and debris strewn and scattered outside the complex's main gate high above. A dark mass of people seemed to be gathering at the base of the road far below. Faint pops of light and distant bangs carried over the silence of Homefields as she watched.

With a gasp she realized what was missing. As far back as she could remember the noise of the Master Drill had never ceased, but now the great machine was silent.

Loa knew the hike to the complex was a long one, but it was the best direction to find some answers. Her legs ached, but she plodded on. It was halfway between forever and the time she left, that she startled at a large explosion high up on the winding road, past the company store. Tired as she was she nevertheless quickened her pace, and soon found herself in a train of people making their way toward the complex. Hugging the wall to avoid being stampeded, she tried asking questions, but the men and women were too distracted to answer, brushing her off with a "You shouldn't be up here!" and "Go home little one!"

"I'm looking for my dad!" she shouted back, but no one responded.

As the store grew closer she was alarmed to see the drop-steel door had been forced open and propped with a stack of metal crates. People were swarming in and out, their arms full with various boxes and packages which they clearly had not paid for. Dashing up to the entrance she peered in and saw the counters were smashed and merchandise from the high shelves was strewn all over the floor. Adults and a few children were cramming things under their arms and stuffing their pockets with whatever they could reach. Loa struggled with herself before turning to press on.

A large hand grabbed her shoulder and she was tugged backward. Startled, she looked up into the wrinkled face of the man who had called for a vote at community hall. His skin was ashy and scratched.

"You're Loa!" He grabbed her tightly.

"Have you seen Marren Dantrue?" Loa asked, raising her voice over the noise of the crowd. "He's my dad! Do you know where he is?"

"Yes!" The man's face broke into an odd smile before going vacant. "They took us all, arrested; we were behind the prison field, about to be sent underground, but something happened; the doors burst in and the field shut down. The guards were scattered. Marren stayed behind with many of the others; they broke into a weapons locker, they've taken over Breach Command. He told me to find you!"

Loa tried to follow but wasn't quite sure where that left her. "Is he coming out?"

"We've been trying to rally the colony. We've got the Gevroh Enforcers pinned between us up the hill, Marren's men are pushing out and we're pushing up, but you can't help here Loa, you have to stay back."

"But I have to make sure my dad is ok! I tried to send help to him!" She struggled, but he held her easily.

"Listen, Gevroh has heavy weapon drops coming in; we don't have much time to secure the complex. Your dad knows his business, I'm sure they've got a signal out by now."

Loa strained for a view of the complex gate, but the rise of the road made it too high to see. "You don't understand, they wrecked our house! I have to make sure he's ok; I have to see what happened... I have to see..." She trailed off quietly.

The man's face softened. "You should get in there!" He pointed back to the company store. "Take something before it's all gone."

She frowned at him, but stopped struggling.

"Your father will be fine! Now get down there and stay in the store. Someone will get you when it's safe to come up the hill. They will tell you Norell sent them, that's me. Now GO!" He gave her a light shove and made a point of watching her as she trudged back down to the store. Catching sight of a squashed Liquing on the floor made her stomach growl and she scanned the shelves for something to eat. Almost everything was gone, even the poster of the Gevrider had been ripped down; though she was glad to remember the vehicle itself was never kept here in the store.

"Loa!" She saw Derig in the back having just rescued a box of Glow-Ups from a forgotten corner, which he balanced on the edge of the smashed counter and tore open. Grinning despite herself Loa rushed to his side and stretched on her toes to see inside the box. Somehow it was still almost full; there must have been eight different flavors inside.

"Orangemmon! I've never seen one, can I have it?" She asked, reaching for a bright orange wrapper that seemed to outshine the others.

"Trade." Derig said promptly, pulling the box along the counter and out of reach. "Got any Liquings?"

"What? No..." She couldn't hide the anger in her voice. "I don't have anything, I could have come in here before and taken loads of stuff, but I was looking for my dad. Besides everyone is stealing. Nobody paid for any of this stuff did they?"

Derig laughed, cramming a second Glow-Up in his mouth before pulling it out again. "Who cares, dad says we're taking over the entire business.

No more Tasking days, no more rubeet rations, no more detention."

Loa gasped. "No more detention?! Is Henya coming back up?"

"Maybe. But they have to take over the whole complex first; every Enforcer got to get beat up and locked behind the prison fields."

Loa felt a chill under her skin. "Derig, they destroyed our house, and I tried to send the... I asked the tall man to help." She felt her face going red.

"The *tall man*!" Derig squealed with laughter, pulling the box away as she reached again. "Skitters, you were missing, probably unconscious for three days; that was a dream, it's not real. I don't know how you got back up, but the 'tall man' never happened."

She reached again more aggressively but he put his back to her. It was too much.

"Give it!" She screamed. "You *never* share! I get to have a Glow-Up you can't get them all! There's no way you could eat all those!"

Derig was startled, but recovered his smirk. "I told you Skitters, trade! Find me some Liquings; these are mine."

"NO!" She shrieked at the top of her lungs, clawing and reaching as he pushed hard and flung her away.

What happened next was a blur of darkness and sound. Loa heard adult voices screaming and shouting, and through a haze of whirling blackness she saw Derig collapse in the corner, shaking like a blade of curl-grass. The counter had been knocked over, and the movement of the crowd suddenly stopped. Like a hole with no bottom, an inky pool of shadow gathered in the center of the floor, and from it rose a solid shape—the dark figure from her dream. It stood with its back to her, as though to challenge the people outside. Loa got to her feet, gasping as it turned to face her, the box of Glow-Ups in its hand. Her eyes flicked to the gawking crowd, and she swallowed as she took the box and placed it on the floor. She opened her mouth to speak, but remembering the Orangemmon she knelt to grab it, and she took a Strawbuzzy… and a Cherryboom. A large man with a portable mining laser clutched in his hands shoved to the front of the throng, pointing it like a weapon.

"What in the will of the Core is happening here? Step AWAY FROM THE CHILDREN!" He roared.

"No!" Loa jumped in front of the figure with her arms out. "He's a friend! He's… he's friendly! He wants to help!"

"What is it?" Someone asked. "That's Marren's girl, who is that?!" Confusion and bickering set in.

"Don't point guns or anything. He's FRIENDLY!" Loa yelled. But no one seemed to listen.

"This is some Corporation stunt." The man with the mining laser was sweating; he looked very angry. He lowered the nozzle to point at Loa. "Step away little girl, you don't know that that thi—" The dark figure swatted the air and the mining laser flew out of the man's hand, splashing to pieces against the wall. There were several cries and the man yipped, stumbling back into their midst as Derig streaked past with a wail and vanished into the crowd. Everyone was backpedaling now, giving Loa and her guest a wide berth. Loa grabbed the figure's arm and pulled. Its attention remained fixed on their audience.

"Please!" She squeezed and tugged, but the wrist was cold and hard as stone. "Please don't hurt anyone. I just want to find my dad, and my sister! She's in detention, and so are lots of others. Can you help them?" She took a breath. "My sister's name is Henya Dantrue. My dad is..." She glared at the wall, recalling Norell's lecture. "I think, in the Breach control, the breach Command room. Can you make sure he is safe?" The figure looked down at her, and she heard the metallic scraping breath. Slowly it nodded, but a fresh wave of panic outside made her start. People were streaking past the store, fleeing higher up the road.

Chapter 10

"PODS!" Several voices shrieked at once. A far away boom echoed across the crater and she looked up at the figure before creeping to the edge of the doors, to peer down the hill. Objects were streaking into the valley through the dome-shield above, penetrating its glassy surface with flashes of light. Their shape reminded her of her father's description of eggs, which people could eat—except these were large and sinister. Round and burnished yellow, and at least as tall as her house, there were dozens of them, falling through the air and exploding into spidery new shapes as they neared the ground. Each pod sprouted mechanical legs that thrust out and caught the valley floor as it rose to meet them, absorbing the impact and scuttling into action. The pods' smooth upper surfaces burst into barrel-ended arms, which immediately turned and began firing up the hill. Loa squealed and ducked into the store as heavy carbine slugs thudded into the surface of the road.

"They're shooting at us! They're going to kill everyone!" She screamed with her hands over her ears. "Make them stop!" She pleaded, but the figure was already moving. Its body melted into shadow and like a dark void cutting through the ground it swam into the road. There was an explosion, and heavy electronic voices from the bottom of the hill began to chirp and growl as the sound of shooting grew louder.

Loa released her ears cautiously; the ricochets near the store seemed to have stopped. She crawled to the metal crates propping the doors and peaked around the corner. The machines at the bottom of the hill were firing wildly at the valley floor all around them, as though unable to agree on a target. She saw the dark figure vanish and reappear, landing heavily on one of the pods and plunging its arms through the top before ripping it open like a rotten rubeet. From pod to pod it went, too fast to keep track of until out of the corner of her eye she would spot an explosion or robotic limbs flung into the air. The smell of electric fire billowed up the hill as the figure worked, and she saw flashes of golden light rippling under the blackness of its arms and body.

The crowd on the road huddled against the crater wall, stunned and staring. Soon there were no working pods left on the valley floor, only spark spitting shells and twitching limbs. The figure turned its attention to the sky as a fresh wave of enemies breached the dome-shield. There must have been dozens more of them. Pulses of golden light were flickering in the dark face now as the figure raised his arms and howled; a piercing metallic sound that shook the crater and muffed into a deep drone when Loa clamped her hands over her ears, curling up behind the crates. With an echoing boom one of the pods exploded in midair, then another, then the dome was filled with flashes and bangs as light peppered the valley floor from the sky above. Smoldering egg shaped husks and chunks of metal with trails of smoke crashed to the ground in every direction as the dark figure stood very still, arms raised.

Suddenly there was a voice on the air broadcasting over the Corporation's speaker system, and for a moment Loa thought she heard her father, but she couldn't make out the words over the sounds of conflict below. At last the explosions and crashes stopped, and the dark figure's howling was silent.

Loa removed her hands and heard a soft murmur of voices from the road above. The murmur built into a roar, and then everyone was cheering. Men and women shouted in disbelief, punching the air and seizing each other. Trembling and elated, Loa emerged from the crates and looked toward the complex. The pillars of smoke above the Breach Pit were spreading, but no sound could be heard above the celebration. The figure rose before her and held out its hand. Loa took it and saw golden cracks of light clearly visible beneath the surface of the shrouded arms. As they turned to walk up the hill the people who were closest dropped to their knees. Many cried out.

"Core be praised!" An old man shook his fists and fell to his hands; others following his example.

"It must be the Emperor's will!" Someone yelled, and the hushed crowd parted, with more and more taking to their knees as they passed. It was awkward for Loa, who looked around, trying to catch their eyes and smile, but everyone seemed too nervous to look up.

As they crested the hill she saw the road was strewn with upturned tasking carts and broken minecars, beyond which was a line of men in dark red Enforcer uniforms on their knees, hands behind their heads. The dust-suit clad men and women who stood guarding them were familiar; some of them had certainly been at the community hall meeting, and all of them were clutching weapons—a few had Corporation blasters or minding rods, while others hefted laser drills or motepicks. They gasped and whispered as Loa and the dark figure approached.

"It's ok," She said, looking up and releasing his hand. "Where is my dad? Where is Marren Dantrue?"

No one moved. All eyes were on the dark figure. Weapons twitched and shifted.

"Don't!" Loa yelled. "He just destroyed all those pod walkers. He is FRIENDLY." There were some nervous nods and tentative smiles.

"LOA!" Her father's voice was shrill as he barreled out of the blackened front gate and raced toward her. The figure lowered its head and stepped back as Marren snatched his daughter off the ground with a cry. Unable to hold back any longer, the tears streaked down her cheeks and she squished herself in his embrace. Marren swayed, clearing his throat to speak.

"Loa, Petal we did it! We got the signal out! The Sanctor's flagship responded and the Corporation fleet has been ordered to stand down. One ship..." He choked and steadied himself. "One ship must have disobeyed and dropped the walkers... We were desperate, but you, and your... you saved us. What... who is he?"

"I don't know how to explain... him," she said, her face pressed into her father's collar, smelling the light dust-worn scent she'd known all her life.

"I'm so sorry Petal. I'm so sorry I didn't believe you."

"Marren! Mr. Dantrue sir," a small, fidgety man said breathlessly, "the crater is ours, and the fleet is dispersing, but the detention pit is still locked down. Sir, how do we proceed?" The man was clutching a tuning driver, his finger stuck to the trigger, causing the red hot tip of the driver to spin wildly.

Marren blinked and shook his head as though waking up, and after setting Loa down he offered to shake the dark figure's hand, but it did not respond.

Wiping his hands across the front of his dust jacket Marren nodded. "Right. Listen, Petal, we're not finished here. I want to find Henya, more than anything, but there are Enforcers and Cordrone soldiers down there, and they are dangerous. Aridonna's ship is gone, and it could be days before the Sanctor arrives. If it's possible… we're going to need his help again."

Loa wiped her face and smiled, not realizing she had unwrapped a Glow-Up until she stuck it in her mouth. Rolling the wonderful taste of orange and lemon over her tongue, she looked up at the dark figure, grabbing his stony hand.

"We have to find my sister," she said, pulling the candy from her mouth. "Can you help us find her?" She was trembling, but it wasn't fear now, it was anticipation. The figure looked down at her, and slowly releasing her hand it turned to walk toward the complex front gate.

"On me!" Marren shouted, and everyone began to move. He cocked his head toward the complex. "Come on Petal, I want you with us, but I need you to stay behind me." Loa found a good spot for the Glow-Up in her mouth, with the stick between her teeth, and she nodded.

"Get these reds secured and follow us down—but not too close," her father said. "Let's… let's give Loa's friend some room."

Chapter 11

Watch Captain Habus Craau stepped into the dingy office without knocking, and the overpowering smell of an immense sweaty man in a small room welcomed him. He faced the broad sweat striped back of Detention Master Orsep Gevroh, who strained to operate controls for the bank of monitors before him, creaking dangerously in a large sagging swivel chair.

Wheezing and muttering, Gevroh was fixated on live feeds of the mining lifts; one in particular. He rolled the zoom tracker with squashed fingers, squinting at the dark screen as the lift, still a few thousand feet above, slowly made its way toward the Detention Center. Reaching for the screen he tapped a smudgy fingerprint on the glass. "Damn creature's blocking out all the light—I can't make bugs or bricks of it."

Captain Craau dusted off the front of his dark keeper's jacket and adjusted the wrists of his gloves. "Commander Gevroh, if we weren't so appallingly understaffed…"

The Detention Master twisted his shoulders around and cocked an eye at his subordinate. "Core's sake man, if you've got a way to keep that thing out of here, and buy us more time, I would love to hear it."

"Well, no, sir. But clearly it fights for the colonists—and as we've just come off two years of Imperial supervision, during which many labor concessions were made, I think our reputation in this matter could be of use."

Gevroh snorted. "Wake up Craau. We're at war, the surface is lost. And your *concessions* have been stamped out, ever since the Imps left us alone. The difference is down here we have bargaining chips. I warned them—I warned them this would happen."

The Captain nodded. "Apologies, Commander. I will speak more plainly. We should surrender. Turn over the children. We passed every inspection, every muster, under the occupation. Our methods never failed to meet the Sanctor's expectations…" But he trailed off as Gevroh shook his head, chuckling. It was an ugly watery sort of sound, like something was lodged in his throat, bobbing up and down.

"Do you know why your access is more restricted than your predecessor?" Gevroh asked.

"Security seasons change, I do not question it."

"Craau you're a wet fool," Gevroh said. "The Imperial Liaison was never deceived about our operation, because you believed you were telling her the truth. Every labor report, every activity log, every class instruction—fabrications. Detention has been decoupled from reintegration. We do not teach the children here; they've been digging! Since before you arrived these miscreants have been helping the Corporation search for the Tomb of Adouras; right under the Sanctor's nose! Every child digs until they can dig no more… Easier to manage than adults, and less likely to talk. They defer to their elders, poor little scamps. A little terror goes a long way down here." Gevroh nodded into the soft well of his neck with a satisfied frown.

The Captain was stunned. "But the classroom disks... I saw them weekly!"

"Doctored my dear man! Classes from twenty years ago." Gevroh grinned and slapped the greasy arm of his chair. "Tokens on the table Craau! Now you know the truth. We can't surrender to the Sanctor, nor the colonists, and certainly not to this... this Star Shadow's ghost or whatever the stinking thing turns out to be. No my friend, they find out we're working colony children to the bones and it's vacuum pods for the lot of us!"

The Captain clenched his jaws. "My entire tenure here," he said slowly, staring at the monitors. "All this time, I've been misdirected…"

"*Directed* I should say, not misdirected," Gevroh grunted. "We groomed you for the part man. You fooled the Liaison because she found no deception in you. GUARDS!" he roared, and two masked soldiers in similar red uniforms were suddenly at the door.

Craau stepped forward defiantly. "All of it, from the beginning, lies!" he exclaimed, pointing at the elevator, a small square of black descending on the screen. "Whatever this is, your reckoning has come. Release the children, I beg you!" and he struggled as the men locked powered braces on his arms, and dragged him from the office.

Gevroh was laughing. "Just a few moments is all I need. Bargaining chips. The monster can have the crutting kids; he can eat them for all I care! Take the captain to the hole. And fetch me Dantrue; in fact bring her whole gang, I want them lined up at the blast doors before I get there. I don't trust our sentry guns to do the trick..."

Chapter 12

Loa held her father's hand tightly as the mine lift plummeted down into the darkness of the tube. The ride was clanking and cold, lit only by the winking of light dots on the shaft wall outside. The faces of the adults around her were grim, and Loa's stomach lurched wildly as the drop increased in speed. The dark figure was no longer among them.

"What do you suppose he, or it... what do you suppose it is doing down there?" A gaunt woman with a black headscarf spoke softly. Marren squeezed Loa's hand.

"Waiting." Loa startled herself, but she knew she was right. "He's waiting; he won't do anything until I let him... until I tell him to." She looked around, clinging to Marren's leg as they stared at her.

Her father looked puzzled. "Petal, is he… a robot of some kind? Do you control him?"

"No, he's not. I don't know. I just know he's waiting. I can feel it." She spoke into her father's leg, hoping only he would hear.

Marren's friend Norell cleared his throat. "Five minutes till we land. They've got us heavily outgunned Marren, when these doors open..." He looked at Loa and back at her father.

"No." She responded as Marren started to speak. "He won't let them hurt us. Will we find Henya?"

"Yes." Marren choked over his answer, and tried again. "Yes Petal. We will."

"But on report days she sent no messages, not… for a long time."

"I'm sure she's doing fine, a little thin probably, we'll have to fatten her up." He smiled despite the wetness in his eyes. "We're doing this," he spoke to the group. There was a murmur of agreement. "We're going to unlock the Detention Center, and make that Gevroh slug pay… pay for what he's done."

Loa had never seen her father so brave, and she hoped he was right.

"If I know a Gevroh the Detention Master will try to bargain with us," Norell said. "If he's heard anything about your role up here Marren, you bet he'll use it against you."

"I haven't seen my daughter in over two years." Marren's response was measured and distant. "If he's touched a single eyelash…"

Loa could feel his hand going clammy, and she pulled hers away to wipe on her dustjacket. She grabbed his hand again.

"Dad, don't worry about Henya. He's going to help us, and he'll help all her friends in detention too." It had to be true, she could feel it, could feel his presence in her head, like a dark dream sleeping in the back of her mind, waiting to awaken. But not yet. She had to reach the bottom first; she had to be sure Henya was ok.

With a squealing grind of poorly maintained metal the ride came to an end. Hushed and trembling, the people in the lift hunkered down with weapons raised. Marren blocked Loa's view, pushing her to the back and telling her to be quiet. With a sudden hiss the doors slid open. Della, the woman with the black head scarf, gasped at the sight, and Norell grabbed her.

"Wait!" He growled. The hallway outside was consumed in darkness, choking out the light from the lift completely. Loa craned her head but could not see the floor; it was as though the lift had opened into an abyss of sheer nothing. Norell began to speak but Marren shushed him, and the adults tensed to listen. There was a faint whisper in the darkness, and though Loa could not make out the words she knew immediately what had to be done. Smiling at her father she stepped out of the lift.

"Don't be afraid!" Loa turned away from them and they watched in wonder as the blackness began to shrink, peeling itself from the corners of the hallway and collapsing into a singular mass before her. The dark figure rose to his full height and looked down. Loa grabbed its hand, releasing her father, and Marren ventured out of the lift with the others creeping behind. Ahead of them the hallway ended abruptly at a towering set of blast doors, sealed and silent. A pair of large heavy monitors framed the doors on either side, angled down to face the intruders. The dismantled remains of ceiling-mounted sentry guns were broken on the floor, their sensor panels burned out and black.

"We'll never breach these doors!"

"Norell, have a little faith." Marren looked at the dark figure, and down at Loa's upturned face. "Well Petal, can he help us get in?" With a pop the monitors clicked on. Grainy and crawling with horizontal lines, they were not easy to make out.

Loa pointed. "Those are detention students!"

In the left screen was a large group of children standing shoulder to shoulder in rows. They wore long colorless smocks and loose pants, with dark metal collars around their necks; most had long dirty hair tied back in knots. Standing with heads bowed Loa could scarcely tell them apart; they looked thin and stretched, boys and girls dressed alike.

"Gevroh!" Norell had pointed his weapon at the second monitor. A wide, grotesque face filled the screen, and Detention Master Orsep Gevroh grinned down at them. Loa hated him on sight and clutched the dark figure's hand on one side; her father's on the other.

"Ladies and gentlemen I would like to start by congratulating you on an impressive mutiny." His voice was thickly sick sounding, and Loa wanted to plug her ears; but more than that she wanted to ask him questions, and make him answer. Marren seemed to share her idea, and waved his arm to get the fat man's attention.

"We want those children released! You can't keep us out, and you can't wait us out."

"Can't I?" Orsep Gevroh chuckled in a squeaky, sweaty kind of way. "I've got 15,000 EMKs hoarded down here; and the collars you see these children wearing are *break-rings*. They administer a mild electric shock when a student has misbehaved... but we can control them quite precisely. At maximum settings I can end every one of their little lives, at the touch of a button. Instant and painless, but loud and colorful!"

"You're going to swim in breach sludge for this Gevroh!" Norell roared, shaking his weapon.

Marren grabbed his arm in warning. "Let the children go Gevroh! If you press that button you will never make it out of here alive." He sounded calm, but his voice vibrated with anger.

The Detention Master narrowed his eyes. "The Gevroh Corporation has been around far longer than any of you; as have I, so you must realize this isn't our first uprising. The only card you have gentlemen is the GIRL." His eyes flared black as they widened. "That little totter there I mean; she found something most sacred that belongs to us."

"Shut your mouth!" Loa screamed. She couldn't stop scanning the children, but the poor quality of the display made it hard to tell them apart. "Where is Henya Dantrue?!" She yelled. "I want to see my sister, I want you to let her go!" She knew the dark figure could not reach the fat man through the monitor, but dragged him closer to it all the same. Tears swelled in her eyes and she wiped her face.

The Detention Master laughed as Marren grabbed his daughter's shoulder. "In 220 years, rarely have I seen a child with so much spirit. I think, little one, that you will find your sister in the front row, third from the left."

All eyes moved to the other screen.

"She's quite the ring-leader!" Gevroh continued. "But if you want her to live, all you need do is come inside and find her! If memory serves these children can be found in tube six, and you'll find the remaining students in their cages below; though I should think some of them won't survive the trip back to the surface. Food is reserved for those who can work…"

"Monster!" Della was white with rage. "Cages?! I was in detention myself it was never like this! Five years of education and labor; severe and at times even cruel but—"

Gevroh pounded a fist near the monitor, leering closer. "That was before we learned the tomb was here on Sekris! These detention rats have been digging for it. And now you bring the very thing to my door… So I hope this creature comes bundled with a priceless bit of jewelry does it? As I understand its will is bound to whoever holds the bracelet!"

Loa looked around desperately, but the faces around her were slack and vacant. It looked like they were giving up.

"How do we get in?!" She yanked on her father's hand. "We have to get inside! We have to save them!" Marren stared at the monitor, and though she was afraid to look Loa found herself counting third from the left in the front row. The girl who stood there had very long brown hair that spilled and draped out of the bun behind her head. She was holding hands with a dark haired boy beside her, and glanced up only for a moment; but in that moment Loa was transported. Like standing under a cascade of pictures her mind flooded with memories—exploring together in the valley, crying in her sister's lap after a dust drain took her token, laughing over dinner when Henya made the rubeets run screaming from her knife, and most of all, Loa remembered how the others had been so much nicer to her, when Henya was around. It was more fun with her sister than it ever was with Keia or Derig… But the Henya she saw now was different, smaller somehow, though she seemed also more grown up.

"We cannot threaten him," Marren whispered, stepping back. "We can't risk it. WHAT do you want?!" he suddenly shouted.

"The bracelet!" Gevroh snapped.

"I don't have it!" Loa shouted back.

"Ahh… then you'd better come in, and let's talk." Gevroh's voice was lower, and cold. With a pop the monitors went black. The nervous weight in Loa's stomach mixed with anger, and as the giant blast doors lurched apart it felt as though the whole world was crouching to spring.

Chapter 13

The chamber on the other side was cavernous, with a high domed ceiling supported by great polished beams that fanned down the walls to the floor. Between the feet of the beams were branching hallways, quite a few of them, sealed with translucent panel doors not unlike the one to the office where Loa's arm was nearly taken... Halfway between the floor and ceiling was a second ring of doors, framed by a narrow railed walkway circling the room. Loa looked down to find there were at least fifty armored soldiers all in black, positioned around the chamber with weapons drawn. Their faces were concealed beneath solid masks; the Gevroh Corporation logo emblazoned on each. As though acting on reflex Marren and the others dropped their weapons and raised their arms. Loa searched the room, and though she saw many exits, there was no sign of the students.

The Detention Master's voice boomed from overhead. "Be advised that Cordrone soldiers don't like sudden movements... You will find tube six through the closest door to your right—proceed all the way to the committee room and remain there until I unlock the collars." The panel sealing tube six switched open. "You will leave your dark ally to remain here—if he so much as raises an eyebrow I press the button and NO student survives!"

Loa trembled as she stared at the soldiers, too furious for tears. She wanted an idea, some way to stop him, but the thought of the black collars made her sick. The dark figure released her hand and gently nudged her as the soldiers trained all weapons on him.

"Where is he, where is the fat man?" Loa whimpered.

"Loa we have to go," Marren said quietly, taking her hand and pulling her along.

"This isn't right," Loa sniffed, trudging behind him. "He can't do this. He's lying!"

"Petal we have to make a deal, there's no other way. We're going to get Henya back," he said quietly, though he did not sound convinced.

Again, the Detention Master's voice filled the air. "Too much is invested to let this trophy slip away; we'll find the trinket later. Full charge! TAKE IT DOWN!" He barked, and the shooting began. Loa felt a sharp and horrible tug in her mind. She pulled her arm free and raced back to the tube's entrance, the sound of carbine rifle blasts drowning out her father's protests. Up ahead the soldiers were focusing their fire on the place where the dark figure stood. She could see him between pulses of light twitching back and forth as the steel slugs glanced off his body. He radiated no pain, but Loa felt a great sadness as he reached toward her.

"Loa NO!" Marren screamed, but she had already caught the dark figure's hand. All sound died away as she squinted her eyes shut and yelled with all her might.

There was an ear-splitting crack and shockwaves of darkness yanked the soldiers off their feet, ejecting them into the walls high above, to smash against the beams like broken toys. The dark figure raised his fists, streaks of light crawling under the skin of his body with almost blinding brightness.

"Wait!" Marren yelled desperately.

"FOOLS!" The Detention Master's voice quivered with fury. "You want them all to die?! I'll give you one minute to get to those children! And take that infernal thing with you!"

"Loa we've got to run! Follow me!" Marren grabbed her hand and pulled.

"No!" She protested. "You go! He won't let us have her! He just wants to trap us, and to get away!"

Marren's face blanched. "Listen, Petal, he could be anywhere... we don't have time—"

There was a cry from the hallway. "I've got them!" It was Della. The others turned with a gasp as she emerged from tube six, clutching the hand of a red haired girl, who in turn clasped hands with another. A long chain of children, murmuring with excitement shuffled into the vaulted central chamber.

The Detention Master began shouting. "WHAT IS THIS?!" His voice was manic and shrill. Norell had found his son in the line and yelped as he crushed the boy in a hug. Loa searched the crowd and found that Henya was already looking at her. She felt a wave of hot tears, watching as Henya vanished in her father's embrace. Marren sobbed and held his daughter's head, his eyes clenched. Henya reached past her father for Loa, her face streaming.

Loa had started to run to her, but something made her stop. She grimaced at the heavy black collars and wiped her face. "We can't let him…"

"FOOLS!" The Detention Master bellowed over them. "You rotten little slags, you weren't supposed to bring the children HERE! GET AWAY FROM THE LIFTS! Do as you're told or I'll pop them one by one and flood the cages! Back in the tube!"

Loa shook her head.

"No," she murmured, pleading.

The dark figure seemed to be looking at each of the tube doors in turn as the adults shouted over each other in a panic. "He dare not use the collars now!" someone shouted. "His leverage is gone!"

"Don't underestimate a trapped rat," Norell warned, holding his boy tightly by the arm. "I'm not going to lose my son again."

Henya was still holding Marren tightly. "Loabee," she said, trembling with tears as she reached out.

But Loa turned to the dark figure. "Please, you have to find him. Find him…"

The dark figure did not move, his attention focused on the second row of doors above, and Loa felt a growing knot of fierce excitement, unlike anything she had ever experienced. Following the dark figure's gaze she raised her arm and pointed at a small panel door almost directly across from the entrance, high above.

"You think this is a game?!" The Detention Master's voice drowned out the bickering and pleading shouts of the children. "I warned you!"

"STOP!" Loa howled, straining to point as though she might pull the door down by sheer willpower. With a sudden roar inky black tendrils poured out of the floor and gathered at the dark figure's feet. The children looked as he rose into the air, and with a blinding crack of light, the darkness shattered. Everyone seemed frozen. Loa could hear her own breath as ribbons of shadow streaked past her eyes like peels of soot. The dark cloud bloomed apart, dissolving away from the outline of a tall figure now burning with light—the gray band on Loa's wrist tingled and flashed as it turned from gray to gold. She could see particles of dust hanging in the air as the figure's brilliance bolted like a lance into the ceiling above. There was a wail and the panel door tore off its hinge. A spray of equipment, wires and furniture exploded from the little room, and an enormous flailing shape tumbled into the air where it hung for a moment before diving straight into the floor with a flabby crunch. Pieces of door and debris bounced and rattled, Orsep Gevroh rolled over, and gurgled his last. The Detention Master was no more.

Chapter 14

Loa crashed into her sister and squeezed, making fists in her smock. Henya giggled and cried, as Loa hiccoughed into her stomach.

"She's done it..." Marren croaked. All around her Loa could hear laughing and sobbing as the reunions continued, with promises that those who were not here would be waiting above. Something compelled her to look and Loa turned from Henya to face the dark heap of the Detention Master's body.

A pillar of energy shocked back to the floor where she stood, and a very tall man rose into being, his shape growing suddenly distinct as the light abated. No longer dark, the man who stood before her radiated luminance and warmth like the golden sky in her dream, and Loa blinked as he took her hand. The man's skin was smooth and colorless, rippling with webs of light beneath the surface. His eyes were pure white and there was no hair on his head, but instead golden designs, pointed and interlocking at right angles like the patterns from the bracelet. His armor was of inlaid golden plates, right down to the intricate gloves, and there was a glow behind the joints of each gilded surface. Shimmering in the air above him spear like wingtips of pure light rose and fell.

"I am the Star Shadow Adouras." He said; and his voice was exactly how she'd imagined it.

With the help of the Star Shadow it was mere moments before even the weakest of the children were delivered from the cages below, and returned to the surface, their collars broken and discarded. What's more, the Detention Master's vast stock of EMKs was discovered, row upon row in high shelves, locked in a security barracks that had been repurposed for storage, until the will of the Star Shadow twisted the metal off its hinges.

"Loabel Anora Dantrue. I owe you my freedom, and my eternal thanks," Adouras said to her, before disappearing in a pool of light.

She couldn't help but replay the words in her head over and over as the lift wobbled its way back up the shaft. Her father and the others watched her with silent reverence, but she didn't look at them, focusing on her sister, who happily accepted the Strawbuzzy Glow-Up, which was still in Loa's pocket, while Loa unwrapped the Cherryboom for herself, having no memory of finishing the orange. She popped it in her mouth with a groan, and the rich cherry flavor seemed to reach even her fingertips; definitely still her favorite.

The trip up seemed much faster than the way down, and once the lift came to a stop they found the Star Shadow was already there.

It was hours before the cheering of the colonists quieted down enough for Marren's voice to be heard on the broadcast system. Loa sat huddled with Henya under a blanket as they enjoyed their treats, watching the masses throng their new ally in the command center courtyard. Loa's heart pounded as she listened, but her mind was fuzzy and warm, and checking the cherry red glow in the dark of her hands, she could only make out part of her father's message.

"... and the cages are broken. With the help of this great servant of the Core, the children are returned to us. The Gevroh corporate machine is undone, and the Sanctor will arrive in two days' time. What I need now are volunteers to queue at the south gate, for help with medical supplies and food stores..."

Henya popped the pink lighted candy from her mouth to gnaw a thick piece of spiced jerky, and she patted Loa's head.

"You're all grown up Loabee."

"*You're* grown up." Loa replied. "You got big."

Henya laughed. "I only stretched what I already had… we had to figure out stealing food, or I never would have made it."

"I want things to go back to how they were," Loa continued. "I hope we don't have to do any more tasking, but I guess we won't get any tokens then, but maybe now we can explore the whole valley, and stay out later. Everyone wrecked the store..."

"I wouldn't worry about tokens or tasking," Henya said quietly. "Star Shadow. I learned that name in the tubes, but I never thought they were real."

"The Empire is real." Loa leaned against her.

"I know that." Henya smiled.

"You missed when they were here for these last two years, it wasn't so bad then."

"It will get better now," Henya said. "Bet we're glad you fell into that hole." She laughed and pinched Loa's arm.

The rest of the day was spent rebuilding the destroyed hovels with dust-crete blocks and clearing wreckage of the pods. All across Homefields the colonists and their children labored together, making great piles of debris and delivering armloads of medicine, pure water, and food where it was needed. Later that evening Loa was surprised when Derig's older brother Alam snatched her in a hug from behind and almost cried, saying he was still sick that they had left her under the wreckage.

"It's ok, I was too far down there, you couldn't do anything," Loa said.

"I wanted to tell someone," Alam said. "But I was just afraid, for my family… I wasn't brave like you were."

"I didn't have a choice I guess," Loa replied. "But I'm glad I was," and she laughed as he sheepishly handed her a Cherryboom, to pay back his debt, he said.

After saying goodbye Loa stopped by the supply tables, before trotting home, arms laden with EMKs for her family, and a box of Glow-Ups balanced on top—the box the Star Shadow had given her; nobody else had dared touch it. She couldn't wait for Henya to try the potato stew, and the fruit juice, with a Glow-Up for dessert, any color she liked. Arriving back to the house she was thrilled to find her sister had stuffed and repaired her savaged cotton man. Loa wanted to help, so she swept the front and reset her white box in its place by the door; she sat Wolby in a place of honor at the head of her rebuilt bedframe, put the Glow-Ups in their new bin and came back down to help tidy the living area, until it was perfect. The Star Shadow Adouras reappeared outside, watching the dome-shield, though he was not too mysterious to nod and greet the awestruck colonists, who pretended to have reasons to be nearby.

Not two days later, under the descending shadow of a colossal Imperial capital ship, her father held Loa's hand tightly as everyone gathered for the Sanctor's arrival. Marren assured her the I.S.S. Ultinauth was an impressive vessel, designed by the greatest Toronian engineers. Loa could see that it was so large that only a small portion of the white and silver ship could breach the dome-shield at once. Jets of steam pierced the air and a massive bay ramp was lowered to the floor of the valley. Two columns of silver armored Imperial Wayguards marched to the end of the ramp and saluted.

Adouras himself was the first to greet the Sanctor, who bowed low before him. As Loa watched them descending together she decided the Sanctor was nothing at all like she had expected. In stark contrast to the brilliant gilded armor of the towering Star Shadow the Sanctor was small; a short, stooped man in a simple brown robe with a wide hooped collar; his hands folded at his waist. He seemed to exude a quiet, invisible power, like a sharpness in the air around him. She saw that the top of his bald head was painted with a great circular brand from which markings and points radiated; dying the skin right down to the tip of his nose.

Loa struggled to see between the press of elbows and arms as the Sanctor spoke to the assembled colonists. Marren squeezed her shoulder and smiled. The news was good. According to the Sanctor it was the Emperor's will that the Gevroh Corporation be dissolved, with their considerable wealth to be put to rebuilding Lantus Crater and the other colonies, which would be *reassigned under the directive of an Imperial subsidiary*, whatever that was. Aridonna and the remaining members of her clan would be taken to Aldaun for trial, up to the severe infraction of treason against the Core. The mine was to reopen, with the Sanctor appointing a committee of overseers from the colonists themselves. Food stores were to be overhauled, and a school was to be built. The Detention Center would be remodeled for living quarters, recreation and creative, and the expanded mining store would reopen, with new and generous options for bartering.

"Everything will change," Marren said, squeezing her hand. "We'll be Imperial Sanction 6, which means new colonists will want to move here; there will be a waiting list."

"Wow," Loa said, surprised to imagine people wanting to end up on Sekris. But with all the changes happening, maybe that made sense.

Several mornings later the artificial dawn found her standing nervously before the Sanctor himself, who regarded her curiously.

"Loabel Dantrue," he began with a frown. "It is not fitting that I leave this place before a word with the one who is responsible for saving the colony, and opening our eyes to the corruption of the Gevroh family's holdings here."

Loa shifted her weight, focused on the intricate belt at the waist of his robe.

"First," he continued, "I want you to know that after hearing of his part in the liberation of the Detention Center, I have decided to appoint your father to the position of chairman, on the committee that will be responsible for the safety of those who work here. I hope you share my opinion that he is up to the task."

Loa blinked. "Yes sir."

"Good." The Sanctor raised his chin, hands behind his back. "So! As it was your discovery and courage that unlocked a relic we feared lost, and it was your innocent need for his help, that allowed the Star Shadow Adouras to earn his redemption, the Empire is in your debt. I would like to ask what I can do for you."

Loa looked up. "For me?"

"Yes. Now that Lantus Crater will be run as it should be, you have earned our grace. What can I get you?"

Loa scratched her head and scowled. Her mind had gone utterly blank, filled with a ridiculous notion to touch the Sanctor's robe and see if it was rough or soft.

"Ondi," She said suddenly.

"Ondi?"

"My friend, his family was sent to Tharsis... I miss him, he's my best friend."

"I see."

"Could they be brought back to Lantus Crater? If they want to come?"

"Done." The Sanctor nodded gravely. "But that is not all you want to ask I think."

"Adouras," Loa said, pronouncing it carefully. "I know he has to leave, but where did he come from? Will I see him again?"

"The rebirth of the Star Shadow was made possible when you found the bracelet. For centuries he slept, bound to stillness. On that cold throne he waited, in the shell of his fall, until he might be reawakened in service of the Core, but only upon his discovery by someone like yourself. Only humility you see, honest and unselfish, could have activated the bracelet, Loa. And now that he has redeemed himself, he is needed where the will of the Core compels him. He must join us in battle to repel the Incursion at Drocia Monor, and when his task is complete, he will return to the City of Rings, and cross once more into the Infinite Realm beyond our sight."

"OK," she said, scowling at his belt.

"But fear not, you will see him again, for you are inexorably connected, regardless of the distance between you. You set him free, Loa, and he can hear your voice."

Loa puzzled with wonder at the idea.

"Now then," the Sanctor added. "Is there anything else?"

Four helmeted heads bobbled and bounced as the Gevrider blasted over a dust dune, careening into the valley below. Six independently guided wheels devoured the terrain, dodging rocks and pitfalls as Loa squinted through her goggles and cranked the throttle to maximum. Clunking helmets with her sister affectionately, Henya whooped from the passenger seat and grinned at the boys in the back. Ondi was shouting to Alam over the rage of the engines as a column of whirling dust plumed into the air in their wake. The box of snacks rattled in its compartment between them, and as Loa reached under the Gel Figs for another Razzmatic Glow-Up, she jerked the throttle smartly to jump the rider over a rising piece of pod scrap. The wheels touched down and she switched the auto-drive for a moment to unwrap her treat. Popping the tangy, wonderful new favorite in her mouth she couldn't help but think of Keia and Derig, and the tearful fuss they had made about being left behind. Perhaps next time they would be invited, but Loa would have to see.

The End

Loa's Secret is one of many stories from B. Lawson Hull's
ongoing Coredawn Chronicles. Loa will be back!

Lantus Crater Map

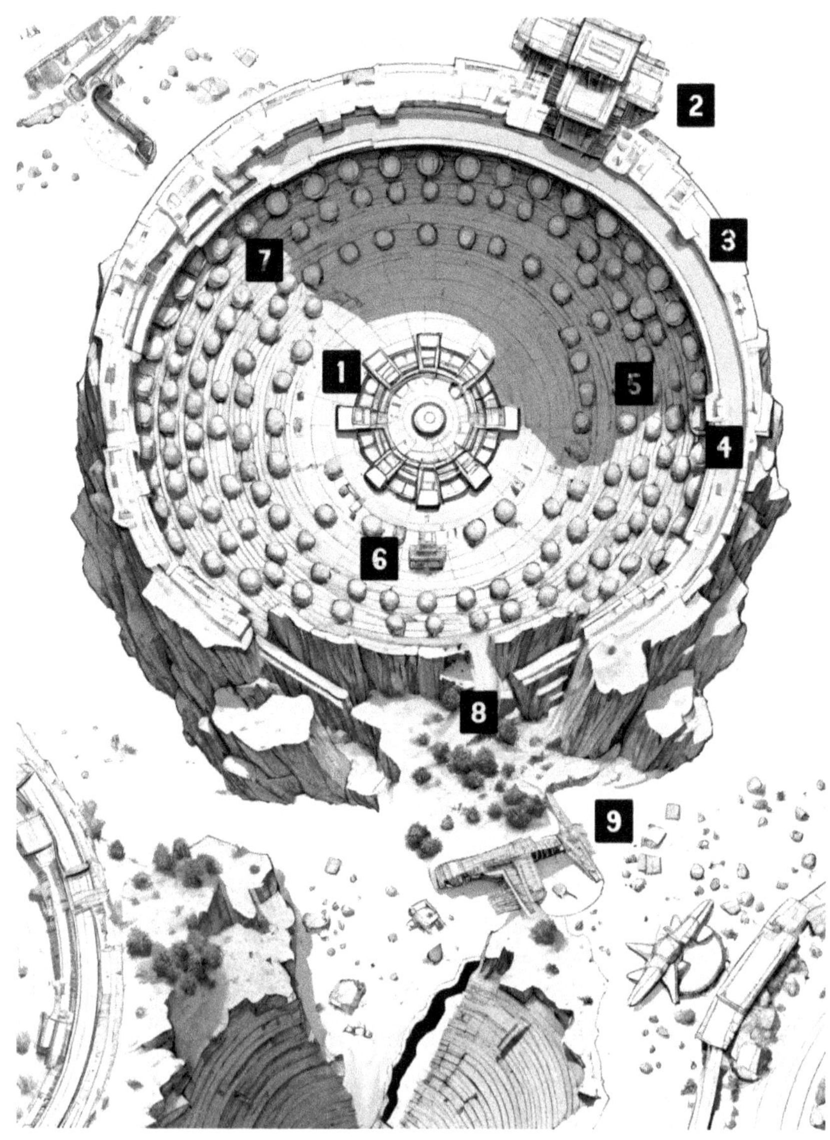

Map Legend

1. Breach Pit

2. Corporation complex

3. Company store

4. Outer wall and crater road

5. Homefields

6. Community hall

7. Loa's hovel

8. Road down out of the crater valley

9. Wreckage of the cargo hulk

Glossary of Lore and Terms

Aldaun: the capital world of the Imperium, home of the Emperor, one of the Core worlds, those planets closest to the Core itself.

Arcidite: a very hard naturally occurring element on Sekris, which even the Master Drill can only chip. Arcidite is rarely pure enough to make use of, and juts of the stuff have to be melted off by careful steering of tuning pans, employed to pour boiling materials into the breach.

Barkrolls: a basic, protein rich food staple. Barkrolls are made from the sap of Burwood trees mixed with a synthetic yeast and coarse flour to make a hard, dark biscuit that is creased at intervals for breaking off "knuckles" of the stuff to eat. Barkrolls are nutritious but almost entirely flavorless.

Beam cap: a hollow durable cap of plasteel, of a particularly heat-resistant substance, used to cap guiding beams attached to tuning pans, to dam up the flow of molten material when aiming the drill-assist melting needs to be adjusted.

Blaster: standard weapon employed by Gevroh Enforcers, its default setting is to administer a brutal shock that knocks out the target.

Breach Command: nerve center for the Gevroh mining operation on Sekris. The planet has a very hard shell, and its outer layer was only cracked at extreme expense, to get to the rich minerals inside. Breach Command is deep underground and was the first corporate construction to be completed.

Breach Pit: the open mouth of the mine at the center of Homefields, where precious minerals and metals are stripped out by giant machines, with colonist miners working to sort, scrub, harvest and scrape at various stations on different ring levels descending deep into the pit.

Break-rings: control collars used to discipline those kept in detention or containment. Each collar can administer a mild shock, or when tuned to maximum, kill the wearer instantly, at the touch of a button in the control room.

Burwood: fat round trees with husky canopies that look to be dried out and dead, but actually thrive in the low moisture. Outside the dome-shield, in the very thin atmosphere, burwoods are only shrubs, but inside they have adapted to grow up to 30 yards in height. The thickest trees are sponged for sap, which is used to make barkrolls.

Carbine Slugs: high powered ammunition capable of penetrating steel.

City of Rings: also known by its proper name, Orovorios, the City of Rings is the site of every Emperor's coronation, a grand floating city of immense interlocking rings that exists inside the surface of the Core. The City of Rings is said to be a gateway between the material dimension of space and time, and the Infinite Realm.

Company Store: this sturdy commerce structure is built into the curved wall along the crater road, and sells all manner of things critical to life on Gevroh Sekris. In clothing the store offers dust and damage resistant suits, pants, jackets, gloves, helmets and boots, with many other mining tools, such as tasking poles, motepicks, hauler boots, laser drills and goggles, most of these coming in adult as well as child sizes. On a lighter note the store occasionally features small animals for petting, as well as higher quality food and candy for purchase, though most colonists cannot afford such luxuries.

The Core: the Empire's mystical central sun, providing warmth, light, protection and hope to the Core worlds and beyond. The Core is the closest star to the capital of the Imperium, the planet Aldaun.

Coredrone soldiers: the name is misleading, as unlike true Imperial soldiers, these heavy bionic troops pledge no fealty to the Core. Coredrones are elite Gevroh shock troops, called in to manage with force what can't be managed by threats.

Core worlds: the eight Core worlds are the foundation of the Empire. These are Aldaun, Rinlon, Gavon, Galidor, Obitron, Phaeter, Terseus, and Sypsus.

Corporation Complex: the large building system at the top of the curved road inside the wall of Lantus Crater. The complex was built up from outside the crater, reaching 10 stories at the top. Inside are mining offices, medical treatment centers, meeting halls, Enforcer barracks, cafeterias, lounges and shops off-limits to Colonists, as well as elevators down to the basement levels and the deep Detention Centers.

Curl-grass: stunted brown grass that grows everywhere in the dust, with each blade showing a distinct curled over shape. Colonists consider it invasive.

Detention Center: a prison camp deep underground for colonists who are found guilty of infractions against the company. Most of these are children, as the Gevroh Corporation has learned the adult population is more docile and obedient, when the company holds direct power over their children. These camps are billed as reeducation centers, where children are treated humanely as they engage in harmless technical labor and attend classes, though few people believe the posters.

Dome-shield: the half-sphere barrier of energy protecting the Lantus Crater habitat and valleys beyond. Sekris has very little atmosphere, but under the dome-shield the air is warm and breathable.

Drill foam: a bulky viscous lubricant that is piped through the seat of each of the Master Drill's bits to ooze down the teeth and keep them from jamming. Drill foam is made from congealed oil waste.

Drocia Monor: a distant area of vulnerable space between the lost planet Drocia, which was destroyed long ago by alien incursion, and the still colonized planet Monor, which the Empire holds as one of its farthest beacons, using the militarized world as an early warning and monitoring outpost.

Drop-steel: a rollable steel screen used to seal off the company store when it is closed. It opens from a ball-like shape that locks at the top, giving Loa the impression of a giant eye.

Dry-suit: a deep mining uniform worn in the uncomfortably hot conditions of mining tunnels. The suit wicks moisture and uses sweat to cool the wearer, going a long way to keeping the deep miners both dry and cool. Dry-suits are however considered a luxury, and only colonists willing to go into debt with the company store wear them. Wages are garnished on credit every week against the cost of the suit.

Dust-crete: concrete made into blocks from binding polymers with dust from the crater as its base. Dust-crete bricks are used to build the hovels of Homefields.

Dustboots: every colonist worker is required to wear them. When new, Gevroh Corp dustboots are very effective footwear, regulating temperature, wicking moisture, and providing variable traction on different terrain, as well as deflection strength against rocks or falling debris. As the boots wear out these benefits are greatly reduced.

Dust Storm: under the placid atmospheric conditions of the dome-shield dust storms would be an anomaly, but the liquid and wind machines used to cool the drills, and the vibrations and tremors of drilling itself, stirs the air such that currents sometimes form a vortex, which pulls up dust in a spiral wall, endangering anyone whose face is not protected. The dust of Sekris is particularly dangerous, containing not just earthy particulates, but metal dust and chemical powders as well.

Dust-suit: a dust proof, dull beige colored body suit with armored joint pads and a retractable screen that can instantly cover the face, protecting breathing. Dust-suits are not available for children.

Dust-vest: a cheaper, minimally protective alternative to the full dust-suit, made in children's sizes as well as adult. The vest is equipped with torso and shoulder safety coverage, with a retractable screen like the larger suit for covering the face, though these are only used in particularly harsh dust storm conditions.

Electorch: a brilliant long-burning phosphorite light source, normally mounted on the end of a short staff which is locked to walls or floors. Electorches come in many colors and burn for six hours before the crystal fuel cells crack and must be replaced.

Enforce Meal Kit: EMKs are ready compacted hot-ration meals designed by the best culinary engineers in the Corporation. Though known far beyond Gevroh territory for their high quality, and ostensibly expensive, the Detention Master has stockpiled them for years, not just for himself but for all Gevroh Enforcers working within the lower complex. Each EMK comes with a tube of vegetable protein, a stew of bovine beef, potatoes and gravy that reheats when unsealed, a pint of mixed fruit juice, a quart of pure drinking water, a spoon, and half a Gel Fig, individually wrapped.

Exhaust Tunnels: giant bore holes that erupt from the ground in the rocky unlivable parts of the valleys beyond the crater, allow the deepest machines to vent without poisoning the miners.

Freezone Broadcasts: a narrowband transmission from the underground Gevroh resistance on Prime, the Freezone operates out of the city of Gengar, a smoky industrial place filled with low squat buildings stained black by the air. Freezoners send out news and updates on corporate injustices.

Gel Figs: puffy little pastry style treats that expand and melt in the mouth. They come in three flavors: Berries & Cream, White Nocolate, or Fudge Dark.

Gevrider: the most expensive prize in the company store, costing 1000 tokens. The Gevrider is a hard-shell six-wheeled TCV capable of traveling at high speeds in safety and comfort as it negotiates dangerous terrain. It is small in size, not suitable for adults.

Gevroh Corporation: a massive family run conglomerate of mining, colonization, and shipping interests. Gevroh Corp's most lucrative holdings are the three resource planets in this system, including Prime, Sekris, and Tharsis, loosely based on the numbers one, two and three.

Gevroh Prime: the largest of the resource worlds annexed and licensed by Gevroh, Prime has several substantial cities and is considered the most ideal place to work for colonists, though the reality is that life on Prime is no less cruel than on Sekris or Tharsis, for those without means to buy their way out of the mines.

Gevroh Sekris: the mining planet on which Loa lives, smaller than Prime and with far fewer settlers, and no cities that Loa knows of.

Gevroh Tharsis: the third and smallest of the three resource planets, workers on Tharsis suffer the harshest conditions, laboring under clouds of haze and exhaust from massive processing plants.

Glodio: a strange little device Loa's friend Ondi made before his family was moved to Tharsis. Featuring a curved wire that would light up when tunnels were underneath them, it was a tool Loa and Ondi had great fun with while exploring.

Glow-Ups: Loa's favorite candy from the company store. These are lollipops that pulse with light from the inside. The light is made with a special glowing syrup, a synthetic chemical copy of the night-light gel found inside firebugs. There are ten different flavors of Glow-Up, including: **Cherryboom** (cherry), **Razzmatic** (raspberry), **Applecorp** (apple), **Orangemmon** (lemon orange), **Strawbuzzy** (strawberry), **Blueblare** (blueberry), **Bananade** (banana), **Villymint** (vanilla mint), **Dewlime** (lime), and **Rainswirl** (fruit cocktail).

Hauler boots: these heavy-footed boots feature powered extensions to the knee which assist joint strength and muscle flexion when the wearer is dragging or pushing heavy loads. They can also be used to assist in long uphill climbs from the depths of mining tunnels when service lifts are unavailable, or wait times are long.

Homefields: a wide ring of domiciles around the Breach Pit, where colonist workers live in dome shaped hovels like igloos made of worn brown blocks of sandy stone. Hovels close to the outer wall are larger, housing many families each.

Imp(s): a nickname given to any officer or soldier employed directly by the Empire, though the term is most often used for law enforcement and military personnel.

Imperial Liaison: the officer responsible for interfacing with Gevroh management to make sure all Imperial rules and bans are being followed, particularly treatment of labor force and maintenance of safety equipment.

Imperial Sanction 6: making full use of the auto-antonym, which is when words have opposite meanings, Imperial Sanction 6 is assigned as a designation when remote colonized properties under a corporation's control violate Imperial laws, particularly in abusing or neglecting colonists, or defrauding Imperial trade agreements. When such a situation is ruled IS6, the Empire seizes all relevant properties, and the offending corporation is ordered to pay damages to settlers and staff, as well as repay all neglected taxation and profit sharing owed to the Imperial Treasury.

Incursion: a word Loa and her friends might avoid speaking aloud, incursion exclusively refers to the dark alien enemies of the Empire spearheading an attack somewhere in Imperial space. Many incursions of the past have resulted in the total loss of populated worlds, but the Empire's fleets stand always ready to take up the fight, and with powerful Corelight weapons, and the increased activity of Star Shadows, there is hope that any incursion will be stopped before it reaches vulnerable planets.

The Infinite Realm: In Imperium sacred lore, the Infinite Realm is that place all conscious beings wake up to when their pilgrimage among those in observable space and time comes to an end.

Lantus Crater: a vast depression impacted in the hard shell-like surface of the mining planet Sekris, the crater was chosen as the breach point by the Gevroh Corporation, being that it was easier to bore into, though according to some they had a hidden agenda in selecting this location. Surrounding the Breach Pit is Homefields, with a long road winding up and around the crater wall leading to the Corporation complex at the top.

Laser Drill: small portable device used for cutting down larger ore chunks. Laser drills are company issue, but tend to break down, at which point colonists are required to purchase replacements at their own expense, or go into debt for them if they lack the tokens. New laser drills cost 15 tokens at the company store.

Laser Pick: smaller than a motepick, these are used for detail work, or "sculpting" as workers call it. Laser picks zap and burn away impurities on rare ore specimens, when gold, crystal or particularly pure veins of arcidite are discovered in the pieces.

Liquings: little gelatinous candies, long and narrow until unwrapped, at which point they expand into thin disks that will float slowly and gently to the ground if tossed in the air. Liquings are often played with for a game, so that whoever catches it lowest without letting it touch the ground has the pleasure of eating the candy. Liquings are a mixed fruit flavor, rainbow colored.

Machine cadet: students of the Gevroh mining program, which claims to teach them all the safety and leadership skills they need to graduate from tasking carts to tech work in the complex, but in reality these programs only teach basic mining equipment, all but guaranteeing every pupil will end up deep in the mines.

Master Drill: a colossal drilling machine, with eight jointed arms ending in gigantic spiral drill bits, which rise and fall, sheering ever deeper down the walls of the Breach Pit. Day or night, the Master Drill never stops running.

Minding rod: a short staff that builds a charge the longer you hold the button; after releasing this button the next thing it touches gets a nasty shock. Minding rods at maximum charge can cause severe pain and even burns. These are used especially in the Detention Centers to keep children in line.

Motepick: a standard issue mining tool like a pickaxe, the end vibrates when it strikes solid surfaces, helping miners to sheer uneven surfaces cut by the drill.

NiteSite Goggles: available at the company store for both adults and children, these goggles allow for night tasking work, or exploring, even in total darkness, though colonists interested in extra shifts that require them are responsible for buying their own.

Petition Day: the only holiday on which no colonists are expected to work, on this day grievances can be brought to the Corporation complex and heard, though exhaustive paperwork is required and those still in line when the artificial sky darkens to nightfall have no choice but to wait another year and try again.

Pierolls: these cost one token for a pack of four. Pierolls are similar in shape to barkrolls, but more like bread buns, softer on the teeth and with more flavor, being both lightly sweet and salty.

Plasteel: a synthetic metal that is strong as steel but more flexible.

Plastin: a molded rubbery polymer that is heated to harden it into various shapes. Cheap and difficult to dispose of.

Pod Walkers: egg-shaped robotic sentries larger than ten people together, the walkers can be ejected from Gcvroh patrol ships to explore possible dig sites, or penetrate the dome-shield, springing open their legs to land safely. The walkers are armed with both lethal and non-lethal weapon systems, and are as capable of violently shutting down uprisings as they are at collecting mineral samples from the tough outer shell of Sekris beyond the dome-shield, in their role as exploratory probes.

Prison field: a deadly charged wall of energy that keeps detention areas segregated from the rest of the deeper Corporation complex.

Rubeet: the only edible thing that grows in or around the crater, rubeet is a tasteless, odorless tuber that some believe absorbs flavors in the air, which can make them even worse, or when smoked, marginally easier to choke down. Rubeet are highly nutritious, despite their lack of fun, and with barkrolls, which are provided at no charge from the company, they make for the only regular diet colonists have access to.

Sanctor: a highly ranked Imperial governor of his or her own sector. Sanctors are wise and powerful, advanced students of the mysteries of the Core, trusted each to oversee dozens of worlds.

Star Shadow: tall immortal beings with veins of light beneath their skin, these masculine and feminine entities are said to cross the stars from the depths of the Core itself in times of need, bringing power and light to their assigned tasks, before they are summoned home.

Steam Goggles: protective eyewear that is impervious to fogging up around hot liquid-cooled tools.

Rim world space: refers to the outermost region of established Imperial authority, the Rim worlds number in the hundreds, and most pay by taxation or into resource columns, for Imperial protection.

Tasking carts: made in both adult and child sizes, the tasking carts are slow grinding TCVs that can carry small loads between stations or to check-ins when they are ready for processing.

Tasking Day: days when children are assigned to work. Those fifteen and older must complete three 8-hour Tasking Days per week, age ten and older two 10-hour days, with those under age ten assigned one very long day per week, 12-16 hours. Loa's jobs typically involve scraping and sorting the tiniest bits of rubble from the breach pit along a conveyor, which has almost worn through the fingers of her gloves. Without her sister Henya to help her Tasking Days have been hard for Loa, and though she can receive three tokens for a good day's work, she normally receives two, for average performance.

Tasking Pole: small adjustable poles given mainly to children, to help them catch or guide jagged or heavy pieces of debris on the conveyor. The tasking poles are magnetized to common metals found in rocks and ore chunks.

TCV: Terrain Contact Vehicle. A classification for vehicles that use wheels on the ground, as opposed to energy propulsion, magnets or hover technology.

Tokens: these copper bartering chits are used at the company store to buy all sorts of practical gear for colonist miners, as well as playthings for children, pure water, candy, clothing, blankets and such extra luxuries as water or air purifiers, pierolls, and the Gevrider, which to Loa's knowledge is too expensive for anyone, ever. Tokens are earned by adults weekly from their mining jobs, ranging from five to twelve based on the role, with up to three bonus tokens paid to children for satisfactory performance on their Tasking Days.

Tomb of Adouras: an ancient mystical site greedily sought by the Gevroh Corporation for their own dark purposes.

Toronin Slag Column: a long convoy route made up of cargo drones, guided cannisters and other various powered containers of ore and minerals funneled through the Toronin sector to gateways leading to Imperial resource centers. The slag column is fed into by dozens of worlds, including the Gevroh mining planets, as tribute to the Empire for protection from outside incursions.

Tuning driver: these handheld drivers are equipped with spinning tips that hold a dot of superheated plasma in a magnetic bubble, used for carving away pieces of ore to find promising mineral veins inside.

Tuning pan: a large concave hanging device that assists in the directed flow of molten metal solvents used for assisting the Master Drill in shaving down ridges or obstacles along the sides of the Breach Pit.

Wandlight: a portable light device that operates on a tiny Core-light reserve battery, meaning it can shine for years, though the light is not nearly bright enough for any kind of detail work if there is no other source of light. Wandlights are better for basic navigation, allowing one to walk in the dark without tripping.

Wayguards: Imperial Wayguards are highly specialized soldiers trained to protect the Sanctor, and any other Imperial dignitaries of rank enough to carry the Emperor's will to Rim world space.

Art of Loa's World

The Dantrue hovel in Homefields.

Inside Loa's home.

The Breach Pit.

Corporation pod walker.

The company store.

The Coredawn Chronicles will return.

For my family, for all the cheers